DIARY OF A GAMBLING MAN

Men called me "Ace" Tanner, but the ladies mostly always called me Jesse. Up to that point when Manzanita Huerfano and I crossed paths, I'd spent the better part of my adult life as a professional gambler. More than once I'd nearly been hanged for supposedly cheating at cards. Well, for nearly all men, a time comes to kind of re-think matters, and I was giving some thought to pursuing a more respectable mode of earning my keep. . . .

I was in my early thirties, and so maybe it was time for a *crucifixion* of some kind or another. For men, we get to age thirty-three or so, and we start looking for a cross to climb up onto.

If there's not one handy, we'll build something of our own. . . .

YOSEMITE

BILL HOTCHKISS

a novel
more or less concerning the gold of
California and based on the
by-God authentic Journal of
Jesse Tanner,
Gambler, Miner, and Gent.

Bantam Books
New York   London   Toronto   Sydney   Auckland

RAP *327 3952*

YOSEMITE

A Bantam Domain Book / August 1995

DOMAIN and the portrayal of a boxed "d" are trademarks of
Bantam Books, a division of Bantam Doubleday Dell
Publishing Group, Inc.

ISBN 0-553-57247-4

Published simultaneously in the United States and Canada

Bantam Books are published by Bantam Books, a division of
Bantam Doubleday Dell Publishing Group, Inc. Its trademark,
consisting of the words "Bantam Books" and the portrayal of
a rooster, is Registered in U.S. Patent and Trademark Office
and in other countries. Marca Registrada. Bantam Books,
1540 Broadway, New York, New York 10036.

PRINTED IN THE UNITED STATES OF AMERICA

OPM 0 9 8 7 6 5 4 3 2 1

A GAMBLER'S LIFE I do admire—
Du-da, du-da!
The best of rum they do require,
Du-da, du-da-day!
The poker sharps begin to pout,
Du-da, du-da!
I played all night and cleaned them out,
Du-da, du-da-day!

I'm bound to play all night,
I'm bound to play all day,
I bet my money on the ace and king,
Who'll dare bet on the trey?

Monte's mighty hard to beat,
Du-da, du-da!
They say the dealer's bound to treat,
Du-da, du-da-day!
Barkeep give me a glass of porter,
Du-da, du-da!
Gin for me, with a splash of water,
Du-da, du-da-day!

Preface

Being one of them there scholarly types, I feel obligated to tell you where I come by this *Yosemite* yarn. My former teachers at Berkeley wouldn't expect no less of me—I mean, if they was any of them still alive. Could be they are. I don't know.

Anyhow, my granddaddy met Jesse Tanner back in 1918. Tanner was a hundred years old, or at least that's what he said. And I guess it was true. Peace had just broke out, and Grandpa was prospecting around

Silver Mountain. That's where he met Jesse. The old fellow was living in a log and rock cabin about half-way up the mountain, at the edge of a little meadow with an all-year spring running from a big granite out-cropping.

Grandpa (Ward Stambaugh by name) camped out there on Tanner's place that summer, and he got to know Jesse real good. One morning about mid-September, when the aspens were turning yellow and there was a fringe of ice around the spring, Tanner just flat disappeared. He took his mule with him and wandered off in the middle of the night, while Grandpa was asleep. Grandpa told me he figured Tanner had gone off to die somewhere, maybe where he buried Manzanita, I don't know. But that seems right. Anyhow, he left a journal behind, along with a note that gave Grandpa permission to do whatever he wanted to with it, provided he didn't change anything that would cause the book to be factually untrue.

Grandpa Ward liked to read books, but that's as far as it went. He hung on to Tanner's journal, and when he died, he left the thing to me, without comment, just the way he gave me that venerable .410 shotgun when I was a kid. "Here," Grandpa Ward told me. "I guess it needs bluing and a new stock put on, but it shoots real good. I mean, it used to, before the stock got busted."

Now, thirty years after Grandpa's death, I've still got the shotgun, and the stock's been fixed a couple of times, same for bluing the barrel and such, and by God it does shoot real good. Furthermore, I decided to work on Tanner's journal. If Jesse's got any kin out there, maybe they'll read the book and look me up. I can't help anybody find Jesse's grave, though, because in the first place I'm pretty sure he didn't bother to bury himself, and in the second place, Silver Mountain's damned big, and Grandpa Ward wasn't even certain that's where Jesse went. When a man's a hundred years old, after all, there's no way of knowing how far he intends to go. And Tanner did have that mule.

While I'm at it, I'd best make acknowledgement to Cornel Lengyel, one of America's premier poets, for the liberal use I've made of some of the Gold Rush songs in *Hangtown Ballads*. I've used them mostly at the beginnings of chapters. Because of space, they're shorter than the ones in Cornel's book, and in some cases I've rearranged the words a mite. Folk songs tend to work their way along from year to year in variant forms, so I've just added some new ones. The spirit's appropriate, I think, to the world of Jesse Tanner, by cracky.

BILL HOTCHKISS,
Munger Creek, Oregon
June 1, 1994

One

LUCK OF THE DRAW

Oh California
That's the land for me!
I'm bound for Merced River
With my card deck on my knee.

It rained all night the day I left,
The weather it was dry,
The sun so hot I froze to death—
Oh, brothers, don't you cry!

I made my way to Mokelumne Hill
To play the boys at cards;
They brought their tin and turned 'er in,
And then I saw the girl. . . .

I'm going to tell you a love story, though Uncle Claude might call it something else. A lot of things were going on in the California goldfields in those days—though maybe there's nothing so damned unusual in that. The times were exciting, all around, and along the way I just might have been the first Yank to set foot on the floor of Yosemite Valley, the first one to see those magnificent waterfalls from the down-below side. I put it this way because it was Zenas Leonard's journal that first triggered my imagination. Zenas, he was with Joe Walker and the boys when they crossed the Sierra in the middle of winter, at least partly because some Paiutes told them there was an easy trail across the mountains to the big valley on the other side. Anyhow, Walker's bunch got to look down at Yosemite Valley, but I must actually have been the first American to set foot in it, and that was close to twenty years later—because Manzanita Huerfano was back with Tenieya's Yosemite band of Indians, and I came looking for her.

Sometimes love stories end happy, you know, and sometimes they don't. Take *Romeo and Juliet*, for instance. For that matter, take Joe Meek and Mountain Lamb. There's a yarn closer to home. And of course we all know about histories where the fellow and the damsel get hitched and figure everything's going to be just fine. Then it isn't. I know one couple in their eighties, for instance, and as far as I can tell, they've been true to each other for the past sixty years. Problem is, they've hated each other for at least fifty of those years. Didn't keep them from having kids, of course, because that's a natural response in the blood when a man and a woman sleep in a bed, at least some of the time. In the same bed, I mean.

I've got to tell you right up front that I met Manzanita Huerfano when I won her in a card game. That's what I said, all right.

And I need to tell you that Manzanita was the most goddamn beautiful woman I ever met—so beautiful it positively scared me, and I don't scare easy. But listen—I'm not just talking about *outside* beauty, and that's important to say. In the long run, *inside* beauty is one hell of a lot more important. A lady who's not right inside isn't worth the tits on a boar hog, no matter what color her hair is and no matter how fetching her walk might be, if you see what I mean. I was an empty-headed young buck when I met Manzanita, even though I wasn't any greenhorn. I knew the ropes pretty well. I mean, I wasn't no kid, not by a long shot. I'd have been lured on by her at that time, no matter what—because she was a stunner. But it was something a lot more important that turned me around, you might say.

I should warn you. I've never been known to be short-winded, and so this story's likely to drift some. Guess I picked up my yarning pattern from Uncle Claude, who was a fair country raconteur himself. That don't mean I can't make a quick decision if I have to, you understand. Over all, I've got nothing to apologize for in this matter. You can ask, if you want. I was a gambler, you see, and no man plays the odds without being able to decide quick. A man learns to set his jaw and turn the card.

I suppose, from a certain odd way of looking at things, the story of my life is worth relating—if for no other reason, so that young fellas won't be tempted to give up on schooling and take to the mountains and badlands the way I did. I made a mistake. Most likely I should have stayed in school. But when you think about the matter, if I'd done that and never listened to Uncle Claude and his god-awful yarns, I'd likely have ended a schoolteacher or an apothecary or maybe even a land surveyor or a sawbones. Claude, he had the knack of making things out of whole cloth and then embroidering them to suit his fancy, and I liked to listen. When I was a kid, at least, I believed damned near everything he told me—even that whopper about how he arm-wrestled a grizzly bear to a standoff out along the Missouri River. All of us boys believed Claude (or pretended to)—because we wanted things to be the way he said they was instead of the way we was afraid they really were. Claude was our hero, not because he was bigger and tougher than anyone else in town, because he wasn't. What he had was . . . medicine. Medicine that he'd got when he was living with the Pawnees and by hanging around with Pietelesharo and Antoine Behele and Fiddlehead Wilson and them other fellas, or at least that's what he claimed. We boys all figured if we could just be like Claude McCool, more or less, we'd have life itself in the gunny.

Sure enough, then, since you asked. Even before I get started, I can already see the kinds of temptations that'll come up. Dealing out words, so to speak, is just like dealing cards. If a man picks up any kind of skill at all, there's a powerful temptation to use it. It's that ancient problem with reality. I mean, the one that is and the one you want it to be. If a man tells his life story, there's an urge to use words to make things better than they were at the time they happened. Well, with words, that can be magic too, like Claude's medicine.

For instance, I could tell you about one winter I spent with O'Bragh on the Snake River, and most likely you'd be inclined to believe me. That's what I mean. It's true, I did meet O'Bragh, but I never spent any time with the old weasel. So take what I say with a grain of salt. That's the best way. Likewise I could tell you about the way the ladies took to me—tracked me, so to speak, and had their way with me, though I never could see much sense in putting up a fight. When a woman wants to go to bed, she tends to be quite direct in her methods. Like Flo Billingham in Oregon City, for instance. I never knew whether I did that lady a favor or not, and since I never met her again, there was no way of finding out. Of course, I did run into her husband, inasmuch as he came looking for me. Well, maybe he pulled stakes and left Madame Flo and just happened to find me. That man's luck never was worth beans.

Now I was a preacher's son all right, just like they claim. What they don't know is that, religious or not, my pa never got around to marrying my ma—and there was some reason to it. But that's another tale altogether, and I don't want to get too far off track.

Let me start in with what happened that afternoon at Hostetler's Saloon & Gaming Hall in Mokelumne

Hill, a gold town built close to the Miwok village of Mokel. *Mokelumne* means "the people of Mokel," you see, though the Mexicans called them the Miguels. Names can tell a man a lot, if he looks at them close. The date was August third in the Year of our Lord 1850. Miners were everywhere, on every gully and stream, and thousands more were pouring in constantly—by horseback and wagon from across the continent, around the Horn and across the Isthmus. The lads would have pulled the Sierra Nevada itself out by the roots, if they had figured gold was underneath. San Francisco was a place where people were just passing through, though the city had in fact begun to grow. New buildings were going up—there and in Sacramento as well, and in Grass Valley and Marysville and Stockton and all the others. Well, I'd been in California for a spell, and I'd seen Manzanita Huerfano once or twice before that, but there was sure no way I could have guessed how the little lady was going to shift my life around.

With my first real look at her, though, I got an empty, hungry feeling that ran through me, kind of like an ache in the bones or a grass fire that takes off in mid-July and blackens a township or two before it's finished, but something a fellow's afraid he might stop feeling. Sometimes, you know, a thing hurts, but who wants to get over it?

In truth, men came to the goldfields for various reasons, and mining wasn't the only game in town. It wasn't by dint of prospecting for gold, but rather by the turning of cards that I earned my keep. Skill with a deck, perhaps more than my fair share of luck, and a pearl-handled Colt-Patterson revolver that I'd trained to glide from holster to hand—these were the tools of my trade. The barrel of my Patterson was shorter than most. I'd had it customized by a smith in Stumptown, Oregon. Some of the lads claimed, possibly in jest, that the mark of the devil was etched on the frame, just below the cylinder. That made a good story, but it wasn't true, of course. Instead, I'd had the smith strike my initials on the gun metal, a combination of J.A.T.

But my big stallion, Berutti, he's the one who put it into my head to ride south to California. Sometimes Berutti's ideas were on the money, and sometimes not. . . .

Anyhow, the worthless hom-bray I was playing cards with that afternoon at Hostetler's was an ugly sort named Jesus Piedra, a former Mexican Leather Jacket soldier who claimed to have served under Micheltorena—and hence was one of them damned *cholos* who, along with their leader, were exiled from California in the aftermath of the grand victory at Cahuenga Pass. Piedra must have ridden south to Baja and then simply turned north again and come back to what he'd come to think of as his stomping ground.

In any case, the world had changed rather considerable since the days of Torrejon. Now, in 1850, by virtue of the Treaty of Guadalupe Hidalgo, California was part of another country, the good old USA, and that mandate of exile was null and void and not worth a hill of beans. The *cholos* and their various crimes against humanity and folks in general were largely forgotten. Most of the people in California hadn't even heard of the place back then, most likely, when Torrejon was running the show. Somehow the stage filled with a whole new cast of characters.

Jesus Piedra had been losing for the past two hours. *Hijo de puta* . . . He said something to a tall, thin individual of obvious Mexican derivation, and I faintly heard the name Juan José used. The friend, whoever he was, exited from Hostetler's tavern and never did return, not while the card game was in progress. Possibly, I mused, Piedra had sent his companyero to rob someone—on the off chance that he, Piedra, would need some additional capital in order to finish out the game.

Whatever the case, Jesus Piedra was definitely not in

a good mood. I sat directly across the table from him. There I was, Jesse "Ace" Tanner, an American card thief of some skill and a man with a certain reputation as a gunman. As I already suggested, I had Uncle Claude to thank for both kinds of skill. If a professional gambler isn't fairly adept with a gun, you know, he probably isn't going to live too long—not anywhere west of the Sand Hills, anyhow.

I knew how Piedra's mind worked. Without a doubt, he figured there'd always been too many gringos in Alta California. From his point of view, since the discovery of gold at Coloma, the entire situation had gotten out of hand. Those days, California was neither Spanish nor Mexican nor Californian—and the new Yankee rulers were hell-bent on turning the place into one of the *estados*. In point of fact, I'm as patriotic as the next devil, you understand, but I wasn't sure statehood was the best thing. Truth is, California could just about be a country all its own. State or country, though, as soon as that happened, then my kind would be obliged to head elsewhere. I've always had trouble with laws and the like, but I guess most people do.

For my part, I studied Piedra's brown face. A kind of murderous violence lurked in the man's eyes—a look I wasn't going to underestimate. He clearly wasn't just any damned fool. Was this the time to move in for my coup de grace, or should I string matters out—allow Piedra to win maybe another hand or two? That strategy might put a better face on things. Meskins don't like losing, but then, who does?

The set of Piedra's jaw suggested that he'd welcome almost any excuse to put a galena slug into me. No, Señor Jesus, he didn't like this particular gringo who'd been ever so systematically emptying his poke, and I didn't care a hell of a lot for him either. If he started listening to his own brag, not even the half-dozen notches visible on the handle of my Colt would be sufficient to deter him. *Chinga!* No doubt Piedra himself had killed several times that many—some perhaps by ambush, while a couple of his victims, according to rumor, had actually been women. Hard to believe. . . .

It was kind of like playing cards with a rattlesnake. But so what? I figured Piedra was mortal like any other coon dawg, and hence he owed God a death. Unfortunately, that's true of all of us. Sure enough. Once again I held a winning hand, and Piedra was out of tin. The Mexican could accuse me of cheating—and maybe attempt to push the table over and get off a shot in the process—or he could wager the last and most valuable thing he owned, and that was Manzanita Huerfano, a willowy, raven-haired and dark-eyed Indian gal who was his by right of possession, so to speak, regardless of either law or common practice.

Just as I figured, it came to that.

"*Tengo una perra,*" Piedra grinned, "I have a little dog. The India—I bet her against what you have stolen from me, Gringo Tanner."

I'd been waiting for something of the sort. Guessed it was coming, and guessed right.

"You want to wager . . . your woman?" I asked. "Don't be a damned fool, man. The injun princess? Hell's fire, you don't own her anyhow, and I can't figure why she stays with you. . . . No female likes a man with bad breath, Piedra my friend, and you eat too many beans and too many peppers."

The miners and professional drunks in Hostetler's Saloon realized what was about to happen and kind of cozied around us—even though they knew damned well there was a chance of getting hit by flying lead, if it came to that.

Well, Piedra was about to do exactly what I'd hoped he'd do. There's a certain type of man who doesn't have a great deal of sense in the first place. Lubricate him with a bit of *aguardiente*, and he's got no brains at all. After that he's bound to make his way on bluster and whatever God gave him to back it up.

"Yengway *norteamericanos* own blacks," Piedra growled. "I ain't no goddamn fool—*comprende?* The

Yosemite, she's mine, eh? She tell you. She plays flamenco—damned good-looking too. She got pretty hair. Her against your whole stash, eh, Ace Tanner? Mebbe *la perra*, she likes my *pistola*, eh? Hey you, Manzanita! *Ven aquí*, come here. Theez *norteamericano*, he wants to see if any of your teeth are rotten, *es todo*. . . .

Manzanita Huerfano tossed back a storm of jet-black hair and stared at her lover, if that's what he was. Then she glanced at me, her eyes narrowing in a speculative kind of way. She knew something about me, of course—things she'd have heard from men at the bar. Word was out, for instance, that I'd recently escaped being hanged for cheating at cards—near Marysville, in the Yuba goldfields. Sure enough, I'd been obliged to back out of a tavern, pistol drawn, take to my horse, and disappear into the darkness. A relatively accurate account of that night's happenings reached Mokelumne Hill before I did—except that I hadn't been cheating, and that's the truth. A good card thief doesn't have to cheat, and I learned my trade from Uncle Claude.

But Piedra no doubt thought I was working with a marked deck. . . . He was hoping I was. One way or the other, he'd probably find reason to go for his gun—since that was what he wanted to do anyhow. For a fella like him, it's easier to kill a man than to admit someone's beat you at cards—particularly while your lady's looking on from across the cantina.

Forcing herself to smile, Manzanita, in a red and blue skirt and yellow cotton blouse tied at the shoulders and cut low in front, emphasizing well-formed breasts, sauntered over to the table and stood behind the one-time Leather Jacket who presumed to be her owner—and so he was, since she wasn't resisting the concept. Affixed to Señorita Huerfano's blouse, I noted, was a small silver coyote face with eyes of turquoise, jewelry possibly of Mexican origin but maybe Navajo. The coyote rose and fell as she breathed. I nodded—hadn't intended to wink at her, but did so nonetheless. Her eyes were brown, dark brown—with flecks of fool's gold in them. Her lips were full and slightly parted—until I winked at her. Then her mouth pinched together, and her eyes momentarily flared dark fire. Maintaining my mask of *no expression*, I found it necessary to force myself to breathe. A curious twinge ran through me, something somewhere between fear and desire.

"Wal," as Bully O'Bragh might have said, "this green'un knowed he was hooked, fair an' square."

And I was too.

T W O

THE WINNING
OF MANZANITA

What will we do these starvin' times?
I figured to gamble, not work the mines:
The miners bring me their glitterin' dust,
And I take it away until they've gone bust.

Ace Tanner's the gent with the ruffled shirt,
While these poor devils are covered with dirt—
With my Colt revolver and sharp Bowie knife
I've gambled for blood and I've gambled for life ...

Maybe that's what excitement is for a man—when a female's involved in the turning of the cards. But I willed my attention back to what I held in my hand. At this moment, as I knew certain enough, concentration was essential.

The truth is, I'd first made note of Manzanita the previous evening—and, damn it, it was partly because of her that I'd undertaken to fleece Piedra. But to win her at cards? Even my irregular brand of Pennsylvania conscience rebelled at the notion, though maybe that's what I had in mind all along. I've met Southerners, men who maintain slave girls as mistresses—harems, so to speak—that society prefers to ignore, pretends not to see. If the proper wives knew about their men consorting with the slave gals, then the belles them-selves were willful in pretense. Whereas they might not like it, I guess there was precious little they could do about it. By looking only where one wishes to look, it's altogether possible to avoid recognition of unwanted truths. Ostriches, hind ends in the air—that's what hu-man beings are. Someone ought to write a book about it. *Selective Blindness in the Human Animal: Or How We See Just What We Want & Nothing Else.*

Get right down to it, human beings are incapable of sustained rational thought, by golly. That's what makes the whole thing so danged frustrating.

But taking a prized possession at cards—wasn't that in the back of my mind all along, whether I wanted to admit it or not? A woman won at cards—kind of a California tradition. Pennsylvania ethics might not be able to condone slavery, but even a drifting goldfields gambler like me could see that this sot of a former *cholo* had abused his slave on more than one occasion. Sure as hell, that was a vestige of a bruise over her right cheekbone. . . . Well, *el que se acuesta con perros, con pulgas se levanta.* Damned rights.

Jesus Piedra shook his head.

"Hey, Manzanita! Theez gringo pig, he's got all my money. Now I take a big chance to get it back. So I bet *you*—you against what he's already stole. Maybe I lose you—then you go with him for a while, eh? *Quiero que lo hagas.* He hump you a few times, a leetle fric-tion, that's all, but I get you back eventually, so every-thing's hokay again. You do what I tell you, Little Apple. Gringos, they all got short stems. Couldn't use the good part of you anyhow. . . . But I ain't goin' to lose, *que màs da.*"

The remark brought guffaws from a few of the ob-servers. A heavyset Canadian, however, dressed in muddy miner's costume and apparently just in from the fields, offered to bet a dollar that his own pizzle stem was both longer and thicker than Piedra's, whether hard or hanging.

"Let the Injun bitch get us both up, an' the barkeep can do the measuring. . . ."

Piedra gritted his square, white teeth.

The miner winked at Manzanita Huerfano, spat on the sawdust floor, and ordered a bottle.

After listening to Piedra, and after a moment's reflection, I decided I actually liked the idea of taking the beautiful Indian girl with a turn of the card. Why not? No question, she was a damned looker—one who had no business with the likes of Jesus Piedra, an unreconstituted *cholo*.

"Don Jesus," I grinned, summoning a Spanish proverb, "*al caballo regalado no se le mire el colmillo.*" One should never look a gift horse in the mouth. "If you wager your woman, I'll be happy to take her in payment. Hell, old friend, I've already relieved you of all your *dinero*. You won't be able to support the *señorita* in any case. For this reason I'll do you a big favor—and take her away from you. . . ."

"Fuck-king gringo," Piedra replied. "I deal the cards this time. We see who wins. Maybe you run out of aces at last. . . ."

One by one Piedra placed his cards on the heavily waxed surface of the pinewood table.

Five-card stud, with one in the hole.

Manzanita stood close behind her *cholo*, but when I momentarily glanced from Piedra's intense and almost rigid features to those of the Indian girl, her eyes were fixed upon me. Such dark eyes—almost like those of a fawn . . . Then, as though she'd been staring at me quite by accident, she looked away, across the smoky tavern toward the Dutch doors.

A young miner, standing behind the table to one side of Manzanita, momentarily lost interest in the high drama of our card game and instead was admiring Miss Huerfano's décolletage.

Then the cards.

Piedra's hand: five of hearts, six of clubs, queen of hearts, six of spades.

Mine: three of spades, ten of diamonds, ten of clubs, king of clubs.

Piedra glared at me and cursed under his breath. I knew the ex-Torrejon man wanted nothing more than to accuse me of cheating—but that charge would be less than believable, considering who was dealing the cards, after all. The question was merely whether Piedra was clever enough to do his own cheating—had sufficient skills of prestidigitation to introduce out of cuff or coat the card that would recoup his losses of the last two hours. Seldom if ever did a charge of cheating hold up when it was leveled by a professional gambler like myself.

Piedra dealt me a final card: four of diamonds.

"You got pair of tens," Piedra said, sucking air through his square teeth. "I got pair of sixes showing. . . ."

With a flourish he snapped his own final card onto the table.

Six of hearts.

"Three uh-ma-kind, gringo. I raise you—"

"You got nothing to raise, Piedra. All your money's in my corral already. Your señorita against the pile. It's been a long evening. I suggest we turn over our hole cards, amigo. Either you've retrieved your fortune, such as it was, or the little *perra*, as you call her, will come with me. . . ."

Piedra turned his card—the jack of diamonds.

At this moment, it seemed to me, he looked like nothing so much as some demon recently escaped from the land of burning pitch.

"So what you got, gringo? Wha's in the hole?"

Deliberately I lit a little cigar, puffed twice, and flipped over the card.

Ten of spades. Three tenners, three little beauties, and just in time . . .

The grin on Piedra's face transformed itself into a scowl. His lips curled back.

"Cheating . . . *no me jodas!*"

"Gentlemen." I gestured to those who stood about us. "Did I so much as touch the deck? I cut, that's all. My good friend Señor Piedra shuffled and dealt. Was it the luck of the draw or not?"

A silver-bearded miner wrinkled his nose and nodded.

"Ace Tanner's the winner, no two ways about 'er. Jesus hyar's lost his filly, an' the gambler owes us free drinks—it's only right, by Gawd."

Piedra deliberately rose from the table, studied the positioning of my gun hand, spat on the floor, turned and stalked out into the late afternoon heat. He cast not so much as a glance back at his India.

There was momentary confusion on the dark-skinned beauty's face, but she was quick to assume a new mask. She smiled pleasantly enough—the kind of smile put on by one who's known numerous shifts of fortune.

"I am yours now?" Manzanita Huerfano asked. "If you buy me a drink also, I will play the guitar for everyone. After that, who knows? But I tell you. Jesus—he will kill you as soon as you walk outside the cantina, Gringo Ace Tanner. I tell you this as a warning. Piedra has lost me at cards twice before, and both of those men are now in their graves. It is not just Jesus alone. No, he has men who ride with him—a dozen or more. He controls his own leetle *ejército*, a gang who will do what he tells them. You are a dead man, Ace Tanner."

"Obliged for the warning, Señorita Coyote." I grinned. "Drinks for everyone—and the lady's going to play flamenco for us *civilized* gentlemen of the mines, sure enough. . . ."

"My name, señor, it is Manzanita Huerfano. Why do you call me Coyote?"

I took her hand and touched my lips momentarily to her wrist.

"Your jewelry—your brooch," I said. "No offense, Miss Huerfano. Jesse Tanner, at your service."

Hands on hips, she stared at me—half pleading, half in defiance.

"I know who you are, Ace the Gambler," she said. "And I know you will die soon. If you try to touch me, Jesus will cut you first, *castrar*. . . ."

I smiled, winked, and handed Manzanita a shot glass, the contents of which she drank off easily, just as though she were indeed one of the boys. Then she reached for her guitar, sat on a leather-topped stool, glanced in the direction of the Dutch doors and began to play.

Clusters of notes suddenly stood out in the air, frail things of colored light. The bar went quiet, and miners and drunks alike, mesmerized, leaned forward, nodding.

Perhaps an hour later we left Hostetler's Saloon and walked out onto the main street of Mokelumne Hill—a dusty thoroughfare nearly deserted in late afternoon. Half a dozen Miwok Indians trudged along behind a mule laden with a pair of hundred-pound sacks of beans, the creature's sides festooned with several canvas canteens. Ahead of the mule strode a pair of miners, one tall and lanky and probably from New England, and the other swarthy and barrel-chested, bearded, with the look of a former Missouri River *voyageur*.

"So now I go with you, eh?" Manzanita Huerfano asked. "That's what it is to be a woman—we don't have no choices? Listen, Señor Tanner, I don't got to go nowhere if I don't want to. You told me that yourself. . . ."

"True, sure enough," I said, glancing momentarily at those nice breasts of hers—and almost wishing I actually believed it was possible for a man to *own* a woman. "You can go back to Piedra whenever you want—or you can string along with me—or ride your own trail, alone. I'm thinking about heading for Monterey. You ever been there, Manzanita?"

The Indian girl nodded.

"*Sí*, yes. I know all about Monterey. South of San José, where I was raised at the mission. Why do you want to go there, Ace Tanner? There's no gold in those mountains, and that means nobody's got *dinero* for you to win at cards. Maybe we should go to Sonora instead."

Perhaps nervously, I touched the brim of my hat.

"Among the Indians—your people, Manzanita, the Yo-semites—do the women call the shots, or what? I don't remember saying a damned thing about Sonora. . . ."

"My mother, she was Yosemite, but me, I have never lived with those people, not since I was very small. So I don't got no people. I remember some big waterfalls, a pretty valley."

I made note of a tall Californio across the street from where we stood. Something told me he was one of Piedra's compatriots.

At that moment Manzanita leaped on me, sent me spinning, off balance, and finally to one knee.

A pistol shot. Then another.

"What in God's name?"

"Piedra! Piedra!" she gasped. "Jesus, he's goin' to kill you, just like I say. . . ."

Well, this child doesn't have to be told more than twice. I lunged sideways toward the boardwalk, dust swirling about my face, and at the same time I jerked my Colt-Patterson from its holster. I returned fire, a pair of shots squeezed off within an instant of one another.

Laughter. Piedra's laughter. Bushwhacking greaser sonofabitch! Damn it, Uncle Claude, why ain't you here to cover my backside?

A big pinto clattered along the street, hooves sending

up spirals of red dust. Piedra, his sombrero bouncing from one shoulder to another, clung low to his mount. Within moments he rounded a corner and was out of sight.

I stood and brushed the red dirt from my shirt and pants legs.

What about the other one, the tall vaquero? Where in hell had he gotten to?

"You okay, Señor Gringo?" Manzanita asked. "You okay?"

"This time he missed," I replied. "But I'm afraid I'm going to have to bury that boyfriend of yours, ma'am. Us Yengways, we don't like being shot at—not unless it's face-to-face in a by-the-rules fight. That kind of murder's legal."

"You own me now," Manzanita said, almost whispering, as though fighting for breath. "But maybe you better take me to a doctor so I don't bleed to death, and you lose all your winnings. . . ."

Only at that moment did I notice the irregular stain of dark red on the cloth of her yellow blouse. Manzanita was holding her side, and blood dripped from the tips of her fingers.

Three

HOW THINGS
GOT
CONFABULATED

Mokelumne gals are plump and rosy,
Hair in ringlets mighty cozy;
Painted cheeks and jossy bonnets;
Touch them and they'll sting like hornets.

Mokelumne gals are lovely creatures,
Think they'll marry Mormon preachers;
Heads thrown back to show their titties—
Wag yore tails, you heathen pretties!

On the street they're always grinnin',
Modestly lift their perfumed linen—
Petticoats all trimmed with laces,
Matching well their painted faces.

With help from a couple of the boys from Hostetler's, I got Manzanita to a fellow who pretended, at least, to be a sawbones— and who actually had a place of business and a painted sign over the door, though I don't figure this particular doctor ever saw the inside of a medical school.

DON PATO, MEDICAL SURGEON,
MOKELUMNE HILL, CALIFORNIA

I have it on good authority that even Joe Meek his-self spent a year at the doctoring trade here in Califor-nia. It was a job Joe could do all right, since he knew how to remove balls of galena, arrows, and the like—and he was long on sewing up knife wounds as well. Take Fiddlehead Wilson, for instance. I actually saw him in action once. Had a real nice touch with a saddle awl. Those who had Meek for a surgeon were proud of it, and talked him up good. The ones who didn't survive, of course, they never said nothing.

Anyhow, Piedra's slug had caught Manzanita just be-low her left breast, going in on the front and out on her back, maybe four inches aft.

"You're luckier than the devil's own darling, little lady. Didn't even bust a rib," Doc Pato said as he gave her a bottle of whiskey to swig on while he sewed her up. "Mighty fortunate, other than the fact that you took a slug in the first place, Injun gal. Half inch more to the front, an' you'd of had bone splinters in your lung. A fellow just last month, that's how he was. Not even one of them Kuksu shamans from Nevada City way could do any good then."

"He make it?" I asked.

"Hell, no," Pato said, his voice trailing off. "Drowned in his own blood, that's what. Hold still now, little lady. Have another snort. The bleedin's about stopped, Tan-ner. Alum powder's a wonder when it comes to things like this."

Pato took the bottle of whiskey and poured some on a rag—then dabbed at Manzanita's wounds. For her part, she went rigid and shut her eyes and clenched her teeth, but didn't make a sound. I'm not sure that I wouldn't have yelled like a banshee. In fact, I'm sure I would have.

In a big glass jug on one of the shelves, just to the right of a full-length mirror, were half a dozen of what

I first took to be slugs. But they were swimming, all but two that had attached themselves to the glass itself. Leeches, of course. That's what doctors do, mostly— either stop you from bleeding or stick the little lizards on you and let them suck you halfway dry.

Then the doc began sewing Manzanita together again.

"Get you a canteen o' pure rotgut," he told me. "You've got to keep 'er clean. If your wife here makes it through the first few days, chances are the body'll heal itself. But if it goes to proud flesh, she's as good as finished. I'm just tellin' you the truth, that's all. And fetch yourself a new cake of yellow laundry soap too. Over at the mercantile. Tie her if you have to, Tanner, but keep the wound clean. I'll leave a little opening right here at the lowest spot—so the cavity can drain. It'll be the last to heal over. She really your wife or just something you picked up? No offense, now. Ain't nothing surprises me. Guess I've seen it all."

"Not nobody's wife," Manzanita said—her speech slurred half from the whiskey and half from pain. "Hurry up stitching me, you ol' bootmaker. I don't want to start screaming. . . ."

I didn't say anything. Just stared at the expert on gunshot wounds. I thought about laying the barrel of Johnny Mankiller, my Colt-Patterson, alongside Pato's head, but decided against that plan of action. After all, the man was saving Manzanita's life, wasn't he?

At the time when all this happened, winning Manzanita from Piedra, I mean, Berutti and I were intending to head south to Coarse Gold, where my cousin Jamie—Major James Savage of the California Militia, as it turned out—was supposed to be running a mercantile. Well, that plan got postponed for a while. Manzanita, she wasn't in any condition to be riding horseback. In fact, when we left the sawbones, she was virtually asleep on her feet. I did the only thing I could do, and that was to stay another night at Hobson's Room & Board.

"Heard what happened," Hobson remarked, nodding, as I half carried Manzanita through the busy dining area of the little two-story hotel and restaurant combination. "She goin' to make it, Ace?"

"Ain' nothin' wrong with me," Manzanita mumbled as I lifted her and carried her up the stairs. "I'm no *puta*. Jesus, he will keel you. I don' take your money, Jesse Tanner. . . . Where we goin' now?"

She wasn't, I realized, making very good sense.

I put her to bed, and she was asleep before we could talk about anything. For myself, I sat in the more comfortable of the two chairs in the room and proceeded to clean and oil Johnny Mankiller. When I glanced up, I could see that Miss Manzanita was sleeping sound enough, although once, when she attempted to turn over, a shudder went through her and she let out a long moan. That was the biggest response she'd made since getting shot in the first place.

I rose from my chair and walked to the window. Looked down on the street below. A band of miners, doubtless already well-lubricated, were standing around outside the entrance to Hostetler's, and I sensed the possibility of a profitable card game. But this night my heart wasn't in it.

I knelt beside the bed and stared at my new possession. In truth, it had crossed my mind that Manzanita Huerfano already owned me, so to speak. I brushed the hair back away from her eyes—and in so doing realized a dew of perspiration had formed on her forehead and around her mouth. At that moment she seemed to me like a helpless child, wounded, dying for all I knew, the child of this wild and beautiful place men called California. The little silver coyote head with its turquoise eyes, medallionlike, pinned to her blouse—what was the significance? Some trinket Piedra had given her? Or was there some other story here? Something, perhaps, that had once belonged to her mother?

The thing seemed almost alive. But in a moment I realized I was allowing my imagination to run wild. *This world keeps changing.* Those were Claude McCool's words.

On impulse I touched the tips of my fingers to Manzanita's lips. I wasn't sure why I did it, but I really couldn't help myself. I half expected a little spark of lighting, but nothing of the sort happened. At least I couldn't tell if it did.

Men called me "Ace" Tanner, but the ladies mostly always called me Jesse. Up to that point when Manzanita Huerfano and I crossed paths, I'd spent the better part of my adult life as a professional gambler, like I said. More than once I'd nearly been hanged for supposedly cheating at cards. Well, for nearly all men, a time comes to kind of rethink matters, and I was giving some thought to pursuing a more respectable mode of earning my keep—perhaps by mining gold or reading for the law or even by homesteading and raising cattle or planting grapevines.

I was in my early thirties, and so maybe it was time for a crucifixion of some kind or another. Probably it's not so for gals, but for men—we get to age thirty-three or so, and we start looking for a cross to climb onto. If there's not one handy, we'll build something of our own.

I'd followed the luck of the draw throughout the Rockies and the Southwest, sometimes "flush" and sometimes "out of tin." In pursuit of my chosen trade, I'd been involved in numerous gunfights and had a bunch of notches on the handle of my Colt-Patterson. A real Johnny Mankiller, that's what the smith who sold it to me called it, and I kind of liked the name. Along the way I enjoyed the favors of quite a few señoritas, mostly of the professional variety, I have to admit. Some of them said they ought to be paying me.

I heard that line often enough to know it was just something damsels of the evening said to their gents, kind of like, "Y'awl come back, now"—or "Don't mention it, especially not to your wife, honey. . . ."

My father was a Pennsylvania preacher, God rest his crooked soul, and I was his illegitimate son by a French Creole woman. Among other duties, Ma kept house for this man of God—who was never Pa to me. As a matter of fact, he treated me as though I were some sort of wild animal that had learned to cotton to humans and had been given the run of the house, though without his personal permission. He never acknowledged me as his own, and he never took any responsibility for me. As long as I stayed out of his way, however, he never abused me. Some of the boys I was friends with had pappies who gave them whippings. There were times when I almost wished my father would do the same to me.

Maybe because I didn't really have a daddy, I sort of adopted Uncle Claude, as we boys called him. From this disreputable individual I learned the art of handling a deck of cards. Claude was a good-natured reprobate who'd apparently won and lost several fortunes during the years he'd enjoyed breath and cunning. Uncle Claude sometimes remarked that there were a hundred thousand ways to cheat at cards and not get caught—and that he personally knew all but one of those methods. His name was actually Claudius Pennyworth McCool, formerly of the Great State of Missouri.

The fine art of handling a pistol, on the other hand, I pretty much learned for myself—when it became clear to me that the profession to which I intended to engage myself required such skill.

Claude talked of heading west, back to Mizzou, inasmuch as "the females around here has all got tight asses, I tell you," and I was determined to accompany the old card thief. To this end the two of us took passage on a riverboat down the Ohio. I'll never forget how the sun was gleaming on the water ahead of us that morning, the broad river flowing westward into a glare of light and into what I guessed to be my personal future and my fate. When the steam whistle went off, I nearly jumped out of my clothes—so caught in the imaginings of boyhood I was.

"We're on our way, Jesse, my young friend—on our way to some great adventures." Claude laughed. And so we were—on to the sprawling little port town of Cairo, just below the Ohio River's confluence with the Big Muddy, and from there north on the Mississippi itself to St. Louis. "The 'Father River,' as the Indians sometimes call the Miz-sip," Claude grinned, winking at me, "and with good reason, I might say. But for you and me, Jess, it's going to be a river of gold. Just keep working with them cards, like I showed you."

Once in St. Louis, Claude Pennyworth McCool fell easily enough back into his former haunts, and his professional life as a gambler was thriving. In the meanwhile, I was playing cards too. Young as I was, there was a tendency not to take me too seriously. But after a time I gained a reputation of my own, and some of the local businessmen sought me out—for the novelty of playing with "the kid," I guess.

Claude suggested it was time for me to buy a gun—one that I'd feel comfortable with. And that's when I acquired Johnny Mankiller. Just in time, as things turned out.

Because it was there in St. Louis, about a year after we arrived—owing to complications regarding a game of monte—that Claude McCool cashed in his chips—or at least that's how I figured it at the time. Claude's body was never found, though. Waterfront rumor suggested his remains had been lashed to a Baton Rouge Express, a driftwood log on its way south to the Gulf. Claude had a way of rubbing fellas the wrong way, for a fact. I did my best to discover what happened to my pardner—and one coon hound pulled his Arkansas toothpick on me in the process. I shot the bastard in the leg and left him there on the boardwalk, bleeding and cussing a blue streak.

After that I thought best to drop out of sight for a while, and I headed on downriver in a canoe. Back at Cairo, I worked on the docks for a time and eventually started playing cards with the *voyageurs*. From that time on, one thing led to another, as we say.

About a year after my mentor's disappearance, I accompanied a trading expedition to Taos, by way of Pueblo, and in the latter settlement of outcasts and outlaws—founded by none other than James P. Beckwourth himself—I gained favor in the eyes of the bitch goddess of luck and came away with more than five thousand in notes and coin—as well as the cognomen of "Ace," in memory of one particularly fortunate ace of hearts accorded me by the odds of the draw. I'm telling you, that card showed up at precisely the right moment. Few men, however, are able to lose at cards gracefully, and so it turned out that I was obliged to ventilate the hide of my opponent—the first of what would eventually prove to be several more-or-less deserving victims. Johnny Mankiller was earning his name, and Ace Tanner was glad to have him around.

By then I wasn't a virgin anymore. Sure enough. And the years started to drift by. *Gunslinger and card shark*—when I arrived in Taos (by way of Cairo, New Orleans, Atlanta, Memphis, Fort Hall, and a few other stops along the way)—I had a reputation to uphold. One or two young Mexican Spaniards with well-oiled *pistolas* let it be known that they were of a mind to improve their own reputations at the expense of a certain professional gambler from St. Louis—a fellow called Ace Tanner. The idea didn't much appeal to me, but there was little I could do about it.

One morning as I emerged from the *restorán*, lead began to fly. I wasn't really surprised, but I wasn't expecting it either. I dived behind a buckboard and came up firing. By the time some of the townsmen began to gather, one individual lay dead in the middle of the dusty street, and another was being assisted as he limped away, howling. In all, I'd fired three times. The second round broke out a glass window in a mercantile across the street.

As was always the case in such matters, the gentlemen I shot had relatives who were interested in avenging family honor. Under the circumstances, then, the foreign soil of California seemed a likely destination, and, to make a long story short, I headed west, crossing the Colorado River and the Mojave Desert, and found my way to the San Diego Mission. From there I drifted north and arrived in Branciforte in the immediate aftermath of the Californio Revolution. And that's how I got Berutti—won him in a card game. His previous owner insisted "the critter can do ever'thing but by-Gawd talk—only thing is, I cain't ride 'im. Bastard likes to trot, an' that raises hell with my rheumatism." Well, the fellow was out of tin, and so I accepted the horse as a bet.

"Where we heading, boss?" the stallion demanded as soon as he understood the nature of the transaction that had transpired. Sure enough, Berutti had a mind of his own—and he could *almost* talk, as advertised.

"If I feed you," I said, "I'm sure as hell going to ride you. You hear me?"

At that point Berutti wrinkled his lips and displayed me his teeth.

By the time gold was discovered at the Coloma mill-race, however, I'd made my way clear to Oregon country. Actually, I was in a bar in Corvallis, listening to Mountain Joe tell his interminable lies. I liked the thief—guess he reminded me of Claude, sort of. That was when a dispatch rider came in and made a point of showing off a pouch full of nuggets—gold from the gravels of the Yuba River, so he said. That did it, sure enough, because I figured that if there was gold aplenty, I'd have no trouble finding some high-stakes card games to my liking. As the poet says,

Oh, the fleecing of the sheep,
The shearing of the shafers:
The very thought's enough to make a man
Rejoice and turn a reaper. . . .

Well, that song never did make any sense. In any case, by April of 'forty-nine I was back in Monterey, and from there Berutti and I took the steamship *California* to San Francisco (formerly Yerba Buena), and then we proceeded inland through the estuaries and up the Sacramento River to Sutter's Fort and thence to Yuba City, in the process actually getting to meet Jim Beckwourth, the same that founded Pueblo, like I already said—mountain man and fabled horse thief, and Indian fighter and Indian war chief to boot, if a man believed all the stories. Jim was apparently intent upon tracking one Baptiste Charbonneau, a former schoolmate back in St. Louis. Baptiste, Beckwourth told me, was born during the Lewis and Clark expedition and was educated in Europe, where he'd hobnobbed with German princes and the like—and then came back to the Rocky Mountains and signed on with Nathaniel Wyeth's bunch and eventually found himself in California. I guess Charbonneau listened to the same Raven that brought all of us here, a kind of Fate, like the ancient Greeks were supposed to believe in. I know it was Fate that brought me here, and now Fate had thrown me and Manzanita together.

I fell asleep in the chair but woke up after a time. Then I dimmed the lamp, bundled my jacket into a pillow, and lay down on the floor. An hour or so later I became aware that Manzanita was talking in her sleep—words I couldn't understand. Slowly, I realized the words weren't Spanish at all, as I'd first supposed. And the voice—it was almost the voice of a young child. From the intonations, I surmised some sort of chant, a prayer perhaps. Then she was quiet, and for a horrible moment I thought she might have stopped breathing.

I rose from my spot on the floor and stood over her. The sense of responsibility and helplessness was almost more than I could handle—but then I realized the little silver coyote was moving. She was breathing—nothing was wrong—only my own worrying nature.

I lay back on the floor, stared at the barely burning flame of the kerosene lantern for a time, and then slept once more.

Amazingly enough, by the next day Manzanita was up and about and ready to go to Sonora, as she said.

"Not Sonora, Coarse Gold," I reminded her. "You sure you're ready to be moving around, young lady?"

She attempted to perform some kind of dance routine but was obliged to cease after the first half-turn. She reached out for a chair to steady herself, closed her eyes and attempted to smile.

"*Sí, sí,* Jesse Tanner. I have been to your doctor once, and once is enough. But let me catch my breath first. *Madre de Dios,* I will have to be more careful. Maybe I pulled out some of those stitches the horse surgeon put into me. . . ."

"Let me dress the wound," I said. "Then we'll have some breakfast and be on our way."

Manzanita nodded. "Soap and water only. No more of that *aguardiente.* Maybe I can do it myself."

"Not unless you're double jointed."

Manzanita let go of the back of the chair and stood—but slowly this time, carefully.

"I think you just want to look at my *teeties,* that's all. *Norteamericanos* are all crazy that way. Next time, Piedra, he'll shoot straight. Shoot you instead of me."

"I look forward to my next meeting with your friend, Manzanita. Perhaps El Cholo will even be brave enough to meet me face-to-face. We'll sell your little silver coyote to pay some kids to dig a hole for the son of a bitch."

"You pay for the hole, then," Manzanita replied.

"Nobody's goin' to sell my Oleli Coyotl. I have had him ever since I can remember. He is mine."

"That's how it'll be, then." I laughed. "Right now, I've got business that needs to be tended to—in Coarse Gold. You coming with me, Little Apple?"

She squinted at me for a moment.

"Sí, Señor Tanner. Indian girl, she's got to do whatever she's told. You going to make me walk, or you use some of the money you won from Piedra to buy me a mule?"

I grinned. "Seems like a reasonable request. I'll be back in a few minutes, see what I can find. I'll stop by the Wells & Fargo and make a deposit—not a good idea to carry a lot of money around in a land where bandidos are everywhere. That way we'll have a stash here in Mokelumne Hill when we need it—thanks to your friend Jesus. I make proper acknowledgment to the bushwhacking gentleman who shoots his own lady friend instead of the Yankee gambler."

"Not my friend no more," Manzanita said as she ran the tips of her fingers over the surface of the silver coyote medallion.

F o u r

Para Sacarse
el Clavo

On foot they through the diggings wind,
And over mountains tall,
With young ones tagging on behind,
Flat-footed, for the ball.

Wait for the music,
Wait for the music,
Wait for the music,
And we'll all have a dance.

On foot they through the diggings wind,
And over mountains tall,
With young ones tagging on behind,
Flat-footed for the ball.

Wait for the music . . .

I wasn't sure just how the stick was floating—not at that point anyhow. Hell, maybe we humans never really do know how it's floating. We just guess and take our chances.

But I could see Piedra's face in front of me, and I could feel the pressure of my index finger against the highly sensitive trigger of my Colt-Patterson. It would do me good, I decided, to blow a large hole right in the middle of the *cholo*'s forehead.

Normally, you understand, card thieves make a point of not getting emotionally involved with their clients. It's the same with whores—ladies of the evening. Emotional involvement is bad for business. With gambling, if you're angry at your opponent, sometimes you don't make the right decisions. In the matter of Piedra, however, I decided to make an exception. The man owed God a death, and I'd happily act the part of Destroying Angel. That's what it would take to remove the nail, so to speak: *para sacarse el clavo,* as a Peruvian miner near Marysville sometimes said. Piedra was a bad loser, and that was a fact. If word got around that he'd taken a shot at Ace Tanner and hadn't been obliged to pay a certain penalty, if you see what I mean, then in the long run, as I knew, I myself could damned well end up paying that penalty.

Now it was time to move on. Where would the turn of the card take me next? God deals from a crazy deck, and we are the damn cards. Had the time possibly come for the Ace-man to turn in his cardboard? Something was clearly working at me, and Manzanita had a lot to do with it—even though I didn't as yet understand what I was feeling.

Don't make sense. Don't make sense at all.

Well, since Manzanita suggested the matter, and since poetic justice seemed to demand it, I did indeed buy the lady a mule—actually a little Appaloosa mare, complete with a fringed saddle and bridle. I thought the outfit a bit gaudy, but my new companion and slave and benefactor seemed pleased. All in all, this particular investment of a portion of Don Piedra's former assets was apt.

I helped her to mount the Appaloosa, even though she really didn't want me to. But with that gunshot wound in her side, I figured she might have trouble, and I was right. She tried to suppress a moan of pain but couldn't quite do it.

"*Gracias*," she whispered when she was able to catch her breath. "Thank you, Mr. Tanner."

"Being formal, are we?"

"Is better that way, you son of a bitch," she replied. But she was smiling when she said it.

"You going to name her?"

"She's mine, *en realidad*?"

I nodded. "Let's say Piedra owed you that horse."

Manzanita threw her head back at my unexpected reply. "Well, Gringo Tanner, maybe I call her Deuce. That way she follows you. What you call your own *caballo*?"

"Berutti,' I said, patting my sly old stallion on the neck.

"Funny name."

"Funny horse," I said, "and cantankerous as all get out. Talks to me sometimes, when he's of a mind to. Well, madame, I suggest we hit the trail."

Berutti took the bit between his teeth and shook his head. But I nudged him with my knees, and he moved confidently forward—pleased as all get-out to have a good-looking filly like Deuce following his lead.

We took the wagon road to Copperopolis, a town at the foot of the range, where the gold mining activity was more or less played out. The lode, as I gathered it, was generally confined to the hills—along the rivers that poured from the melting snows of a long range of granite mountains the Indians called Inyo and the whites called Sierra Nevada. A great deal of the high country, at that time, was as yet unexplored. One Miwok fellow I'd done a bit of drinking with insisted that a great spirit, Olelbis, lived back in the mountains. Any human being that got too close to his hideout was supposed to die on the spot. What I'd already learned for certain, however, was that the mountains were populated by grizzly bears, black bears, pumas, wolves, coyotes, and wolverines. The higher peaks held their snow throughout the long summers, and rivers like the Yuba, American, Mokelumne, Stanislaus, Merced, and Kings ran clear green and cold to the broad plain of the San Joaquin and Sacramento Valley.

From there I figured to head south on down the San Joaquin toward Fresno River and thence upstream, back into the hills and to the little community of Coarse Gold, where, as I said before, I hoped to see my cousin, Jamie Savage—a bit of a big shot, according to what I'd heard. On the other hand, it was altogether possible that this particular James Savage wasn't my cousin at all, even if all the pieces to the puzzle did seem to fit. I more or less knew that Jim had left Pennsylvania and made it all the way out to California, just as I had. He'd been lucky enough to go to normal school, and after that took a commission with the Pennsylvania Regulars, so the military background was right—and would have put him into position to pick up with the California Militia. As for the trading post that Jimmy was supposed to be running, why, that didn't exactly sound like the kind of thing a gentleman farmer type would be doing, but in the mining regions of California, how many options were there? If a Yank didn't dig for gold or hunt for meat for those that did, or if he didn't skim the cream by means of playing cards, the way I'd been doing, or set up as a doctor or a legal man, maybe the only thing left was to tend store.

Time would tell. If this particular Savage turned out to be the right Savage, fine and dandy. If not, at least my curiosity would be satisfied. As things were, I figured it worth my while to check out a possible relative. In truth, I didn't have much in the way of family. Allies are hard to come by.

Perhaps that was a good part of the attraction I knew I was feeling toward this skinny, long-haired Indian girl who'd become, at least for a time, my charge. What does a tinhorn gringo do with a lady he's won in a card game? You might say there's a certain responsibility comes with the holding of the victorious hand.

Then, of course, there was the small matter of that tremendous feeling of attraction I felt toward her—almost beyond my conscious will, and certainly beyond my good sense. Maybe it was true, as professional gals insisted, that the male of the human species only has enough blood for one organ at a time. But what I was feeling, and I knew it damned well, wasn't just that. Had something to do with 'er, though. Sure enough.

Everything was going wrong that could possibly go wrong. Deuce threw a shoe, and the main cinch belt on the mare's saddle tore out and had to be repaired. Those and a few other damned things. Anyhow, we managed no more than twenty miles by sundown. Not quite to the valley floor as yet, we turned off the main trail and found a likely campsite a short way down one of the Calaveras River's tributary creeks. Cosgrove Creek, most likely—Pete at the livery in Mokelumne Hill had told me we'd come to it after a spell. Anyhow, the stream was lined with sixty-foot-tall alders, and lush grass, just turning to golden with the season, grew to either side. A few of the alders were cloaked with grapevines, providing a nesting area for a couple dozen vultures. The big black birds had already settled in for the night and were somewhat suspicious and annoyed by the presence of two humans and two horses and a pair of pack mules. A few of the buzzards hopped from limb to limb in agitation, while one or two stretched out their necks and hissed.

In truth, your vulture can't do much better than that. No voice box, you see. I wouldn't exactly call them death birds, but they sure as hell have an instinct for finding cadavers; human or varmint, it don't make no difference. Almost the way I do for finding a card game or some other kind of trouble.

Manzanita eased herself out of the saddle, stood

next to Deuce for a long moment, and then dropped the mare's reins. The Appaloosa, for her part, began to graze at a thick clump of grass. Berutti, I noted, just stood there and watched her. Well, stallions are that way.

Grasshoppers flew with each step as Manzanita approached me. At one point she shielded her eyes and at the same time burst into laughter.

"The little men are not sure whether they want to fly away from me or attack me," she said. "They are very confused insects, *confundido*. So, Señor Tanner, thees is where we will sleep for the night? A lesser man might have taken me to a hotel. I do not know what you expect of me—the wound I take in your place, it has made me like an eighty-year-old *criada*. Perhaps I can boil some dried beans for you. You would like that, yes?"

I laughed. "Wounded kids don't have to do anything. As matters turn out, I'm a skilled chef, a genuine *cocinero*. For this reason, Madame Sickling, Manzanita the little apple, you must allow me to boil the beans and so forth. I'll even gather the firewood. Since you have saved my life, I'm obliged to be your servant."

"Maybe we're even, then? You win me at cards, and I save you from getting shot by Jesus."

"Not sure that calculates, little applesauce. Piedra, after all, is your companyero. And a good friend he is too, but a dead friend the next time I run afoul of him."

"Pretty good with your *pistola*, eh, gringo? You got to be fast to face down Jesus Piedra."

"Madame Huerfano," I said, "I am indeed the fastest gun in all of California. God himself taught me to shoot. Piedra will become as silent as the rock he was named for. I'll even pay for his burial."

"Lots of talk, that's all. All right, then. I permit you to fix dinner for me. Beans *e venado, sí?*"

"*Sí,*" I replied. "Speak *inglés*, damn it. You talk Boston as well as I do, more or less."

"Maybe I do," she replied, first frowning at me and then grinning like a fool. "I'll gather the firewood— that is the woman's task. You tend to our animals, and when you finish, I will have enough fuel for our cooking fire. Perhaps I have to light it for you? Then you can be the *cocinero*, like you say. Only the man knows the proper way to cook venison. I will watch how you do it, and that way I will learn. How do you Yankees say—*hokay*? Will that be hokay, Jesse Tanner?"

"Why not?" I said, turning to take care of Berutti and Deuce. If I was curt with her, it was because I was feeling an immense sense of confusion. Was she toying with me? Playing the role of a little wife?

If ye owns her, kay-hoona, then why not just bed 'er and get it over with? As for the leetle bullet hole, why, ye wouldn't want her to enjoy the love-humping anyhow, would ye? If the ladies ever starts to enjoy humpin', why that'll be the end o' the world.

Whose voice had spoken to me, I hadn't the slightest idea. Just my imagination. That and nothing more.

After we ate, Manzanita used some of the gauze and ointment the doc had given us and changed the dressing on her bullet wound. I offered to help, but she insisted she could handle matters herself, and so I didn't insist.

I built a good fire, and the two of us sat there, opposite one another, and drank coffee.

"Yankees all make their campfires too big," Manzanita observed. "You want it to get loose and set the woods on fire? Dry grass, it burns like gunpowder."

"The burning question, *cuestión candente.*" I laughed. "When an American builds a campfire, it's because he wants both heat and light. But we take precautions. Things are tinder dry, I admit it. . . ."

"If the campfire is too big, it is much easier to see— and the odor of smoke and cooking travel much farther.

It is like inviting people to come in to your camp, Ace Tanner."

Off in the summer darkness, a screech owl trilled—then a second time—and then the night was quiet once more.

We talked for a long while that night—talked of all sorts of things. I suppose we had, both of us, finally begun to feel at ease with one another. We talked the way people will when they're fairly certain they'll not be together too much longer—and so it's all right to speak of private matters, of things they suppose will never have any consequence.

"Little brother, *hermanito*." Manzanita laughed suddenly, pointing into the shadows beyond the firelight.

I glanced up, and sure enough, half a dozen coyotes, perhaps more, were watching us—whether in hope that we might toss them some bits of venison or in annoyance that we'd encamped at one of their nightly mousing sites or merely in curiosity, I couldn't say. Manzanita turned to me, her eyes silently asking permission. Then she rose, gathered a few scraps from our evening meal, and took three or four steps toward the luminous yellow eyes. At this human movement, most of the creatures shrank back into darkness, as though they had vanished into space itself, but one pair of eyes remained visible, unblinking.

"Cousin of the brush," Manzanita called softly. "It's good to see you tonight. We will not stay long—just until morning. After that you may have our campsite to yourself. Here is a little something for you to eat, *provisiones*. . . ."

With her good arm, she used an underhand motion to toss the scraps toward the edge of the firelight.

The remaining coyote did not stir—remained motionless for a few moments. Then the creature came forward, as though reassured, sniffed at the offerings, and mouthed a strip of deer fat. The bushy tail wagged rapidly. The coyote swallowed the morsel, picked up a few more things without chewing or swallowing, turned and disappeared into the darkness.

"I'll be damned," I said. "The brush wolf acted as though you two were acquaintances. . . ."

Manzanita returned to her resting place across the fire from me and sat back down.

"Ace Tanner, *sí*. In a manner of speaking, we know one another. I have special medicine with coyotes, and that is why I wear the amulet, my little silver and turquoise coyote. He protects me. The medallion allows him to know who I am. Sometimes we do not see one another for a time, and he might forget. For my people, the people I was born to, Oleli Coyote is a very important person. In some ways he is like the crucified Jesus. The coyote, he created human people, but he does not do anything to save them. I do not know the stories very well because I was still very young when I was taken to the mission to live, but I think that my people believe that everyone has a soul that goes on to the next world, to the camp on the other side of the sky, beyond the great crashing boulders. Do the Americanos not know of this? The priests at San José Mission, they didn't know—or wouldn't admit that they did. They believe Oleli Coyote is a very bad person—that we should not listen to what he says. But I never believed their words, those priests, though most of them were very kind to me. In the Holy Book, the Christ God never says such a thing. There must not have been any coyotes where Joseph and Mary lived."

"The Holy Land," I nodded. "Halfway around the world from here. But they have little wolves called jackals. Never saw one, but I guess they're like coyotes, look much the same. Wild dogs . . . I always guessed that maybe some early explorers, maybe someone far back before Chris Columbus, brought a few of 'em over here."

Manzanita nodded, smiled—like a little kid, it seemed to me.

"I know about Columbo," she said. "We learned

about *historia* at the mission—and other things too, the *inglés lengua, latín* for the mass, even poetry and *aritmética*. But you must not imagine that Oleli Coyote came from some other world. He has always been here. And this is where the people were first created, also. I think the *españols* and the Bostons come from people who went across the water long ago, just as the stories say, and now they have come back."

"You amaze me—a whole new theory of history. But the missions—they were closed, so to speak, years ago, and—"

"*Sí*, and no longer did the priests send out riders to find Indian children—to steal them or to buy them from their parents. Sometimes things were very hard in the Indio villages, and if there were too many children to feed, and if there was not enough food, the mission priests would buy these little ones and raise them as their own. But that's not what happened to me. Do you really wish to hear about all this, Mr. Jesse Tanner?"

Manzanita was feeling a hell of a lot more confident of herself. I could tell that much.

"Of course, of course. So how'd you end up at the mission?" I asked, leaning back against Berutti's saddle and lighting a *cigarro*—offering one to Manzanita as well.

"Women do not smoke," she said, shaking her head.

"Ain't no one around here to turn you in to the mission priests," I said, puffing away.

"Then let me try yours. I will see if I like it."

I handed the cigar to Manzanita, who held it between the fingertips of both hands and puffed cautiously. She nodded, handed the stogie back to me.

"It is all right," she said, "but it is not really good. The taste, I mean. And it makes my eyes water. Why do men like these things? You do not smoke for prayer, but because you enjoy it?"

"Something like that," I said.

"Men also drink far too much whiskey—whenever they can get it. The same with wine."

"Men are devils, all right," I laughed. "Worthless as hell."

I rose, took Manzanita's tin cup, and filled it with coffee from my old blue-speckled pot. I winked at her and put in an extra dollop of honey and then, after a moment, skimmed off the melted comb and handed her the container.

She took a sip, smiled, and said, "You are being a *cortés*. I must be tiresome to you. Perhaps we should sleep. Even though I was careful a little while ago, I think I hurt myself when I threw the scraps to Oleli and his friends."

"Whatever you wish. But if you're up to 'er, I'd be proud to listen. Gal, I think you're teasing me. A gambler does that too—to lure his opponent into over-betting."

I put my hands behind my head and stared at the stars. The summer night was warm and pleasant, and I felt strangely at ease with myself and with the world around me. For a moment I caught a vision of Jesse Tanner as an aged man, and when I looked across the room of the house I was living in to see who my wife was, well, it was Manzanita herself.

Gawddamn foolish idjit. Ye've gone an' fell in love, and not a bit o' reason to 'er. . . .

"I would not tease you." Manzanita laughed. "You're a very strange man. You say strange things. All right, then. This is what happened to me: I was seven years old, and my two brothers and I went with my mother and father on our way to the San Joaquin River. We were following the river of the Tuolumne, and that was where it happened. Only my family went that time, but I do not know why. Mostly I remember moving about with everyone from our village. We changed our village several times each year, you see—to fish, to gather acorns, to hunt for deer in the mountains, in a place where there are waterfalls and great cliffs, that kind of thing. Sometimes I remember it clearly, but other times I suppose it must be a dream, a place that lives only in my mind. But on this occasion my family was approached by Californio vaqueros, and they attempted to make gifts so that my mother would have intercourse with them. My mother was a very pretty woman, Ace Tanner. My father tried to explain that the Yosemite, my people, do not do such a thing—not with strangers, I mean, not for money. The *caballeros* became angry, and one man shot my father and killed him. My mother struck at another with her knife, and the Californios killed her as well. My brothers and I ran away to hide, but the men found me. They spoke of raping me and killing me too, but the older man, Arturo Esquivel was his name, he saw that I was wearing the coyote amulet, and he would not allow the others to harm me. Arturo was a very kind man and had children of his own. He took me to the San José Mission, and there the priests gave me a home."

"Holy Christ," I whispered. "How long ago was that?"

"I am twenty years old. Thirteen years ago that happened, in the year of 1837. And so I lived at the mission and went to school with the other Indio children who where there. Sometimes I thought to escape, to ride away and return to Chief Tenieya's village, where I still must have aunts and uncles and cousins. Perhaps my brothers even found their way home, I do not know. Or perhaps they were killed by the Chowchillas—or captured by them and forced to live there."

I nodded, puffed again on the *cigarro*. "And you have never been back to your own people, the Yosemites?"

"Never in all these years. But one day I will certainly go there. Perhaps you will take me there, Ace Tanner? To the *Uzmati* people, the Grizzlies?"

I thought about the possibility for a moment. "How would we find 'em?"

"Chief Tenieya is well known to the gringos," Manzanita replied. "His village might be anywhere, but I have learned that there's always someone who knows. If an eagle flies from her nest, there is always someone who has seen it happen."

"Not back in the Sierra. The range is too damned big, and not enough people to keep an eye on everything that happens. I just hear rumors—the kind of talk that spreads all over the mining region. But Tenieya's something of a mystery. One old boy claims he's a ghost Injun—he and his people together. They can just vanish whenever they want to."

Manzanita drank the last of her honey-laced coffee and set the cup to one side.

"Only a child would believe such a thing. Will you mind if I go to sleep now? *Tengo fatiga.*"

"Of course, Little Apple. You in pain from the bullet wound? Can I do anything?"

She shook her head.

"One more question, though. This is the big one. How'd you end up with a sonofabitch like Jesus Piedra?"

"Oh, that. I will speak the truth. I met him at the marketplace near the mission. I was sixteen years old then, and he was wearing a uniform. We met several times, and then the priests found out about our friendship. He was not always the way he is now. He was handsome, Ace Tanner, and I was young—even though that was but four years ago. Much has happened. He has changed since the *norteamericanos* have come to California."

"You ran away with him?"

"*Sí,* that is what I did. Afterward I discovered he was a highwayman, an outlaw, like Murietta. There is a gang of men who follow him. I thought I was in love, but then I learned that Jesus, he already has two wives before me. But I am just Indio, after all, and I must not expect too much out of life. Jesus feeds me well and buys me clothes to wear. Also he gave me a very fine guitar. He is not a completely bad man, Ace Tanner."

"What about the tall one—your boyfriend's buddy? How do things stand between the two of them? Are they brothers, or what?"

"Juan José Raymondo Garcia, that is his name. He has been with Jesus for a long time. They might be cousins, Señor Tanner, I do not know. There was never any reason to ask, so I didn't. Juan José and Jesus are very close friends. They have ridden many trails together."

"And stolen many horses together?"

I stared at Manzanita across the dwindling campfire. Even in the dimming light, the silver and turquoise of the coyote around her neck appeared to gleam with an almost supernatural radiance.

Then the night flooded over us, and we slept.

Five

A THEFT OF BEAUTY

Oh my darling, oh my darling,
Oh my darling Clementine,
You are lost and gone forever,
Dreadful sorry, Clementine.

Then the miner, Forty-Niner,
Soon began to peak and pine,
Thought he oughter jine his daughter;
Now he's with his Clementine.

In my dreams she still doth haunt me,
Robed in garments soaked in brine,
Though in life I used to hug her,
Now she's dead, I draw the line.

I rose early that morning. Something wasn't right, and I knew it. Even Berutti, philosophical stallion that he was, was acting fidgety as the devil, and little Deuce seemed uneasy as well.

Somewhere, off among the considerable white oaks that grew near the stream we were encamped upon, a couple of blue jays were yelling their heads off. Blue jays spend half their lives warning about one thing or another, you understand, and no doubt I should have paid more attention. Mostly, blue jays warn other animals that humans are in the vicinity. I didn't take into account that the warning might apply to human varmints as well.

Manzanita was still sleeping soundly under her robes, and I determined to let her continue. However sprightly her tongue had proven to be, I knew she was fighting off the effects of Piedra's galena. When a wound like that turns to gangrene, it's a slippery slope to hell—with pain and raging madness along the way. I sure didn't want anything like that to happen. True, Manzanita showed no signs of turning in such a direction, but . . . well, it just seemed best to let her sleep for another hour or two. She'd been through a lot on account of me. Fate's a crazy stew. The ancient Greeks, they believed in Zeus and the rest of those thieves who'd look down and see that a person was happy, and sure enough, it was time to toss some lightning. Disease or pistol ball, it didn't matter none, except that the Greeks didn't have pistols, and neither did their gods. In the meanwhile, the boys and girls from Olympus didn't follow any rules beyond what pleased them. You read a book called *The Iliad*, and you'll see what I mean. Maybe the problem was that they didn't have anything really important to do, so they just had love affairs with the humans and in general complicated the lives of their little playthings.

I guess that after Christianity got started, Zeus must have had a turn of heart, so to speak, and He changed His name and got Him a conscience—though for all of that, I don't see that the world's much better off. Human nature, at least, hasn't changed much, and the race still isn't necessarily to the swift—any more than honesty's the best policy, and so forth. Take the story of Job, for instance. That's in the Bible too, ain't it? Cunning, a good bluff, some common sense, and a private code of honor—those are things that go a long way toward making the stick float right, if you see what I mean.

I know, of course, that Job's in the Bible. I was "jest astin' a rhetoric," as we say in the gambling trade. I do, anyhow.

But let's stick to the subject here. Take Manzanita, for instance. She clearly deserved a lot better than what the Old Man had given her up to this point in her life. No doubt about it—she deserved better. She needed the right man.

I used the comb and brush on Berutti, and my mare-humper seemed to enjoy it more than was usually the case. I could tell he had something on his mind.

"You thinking about marrying her, boss? That the bone you're chewing on? Then you'll settle down and raise chickens, I suppose, and after that you and I won't ever have any more adventures—until that Billingham fella comes gunning for you for diddling his wife. Then maybe things'll get interesting again. . . ."

I glanced at Berutti, who'd turned his head back toward me—as though he were thinking of nipping my sleeve and the flesh underneath the cloth as well.

"If I raise chickens, my friend, at least you'll have plenty of corn and oats. But if I were to take on a lady—on a permanent basis, I mean—I suppose that would entail settling. Unless the two of us decided to rob stagecoaches, that is. You and I, that's what I'm saying."

"A lot more certain than poker and monte," Berutti muttered as he snuffled about for some grass with just the right taste.

"My friend, you'd complain if they hanged you with a new rope. Besides, I saw you admiring little Deuce over there. You don't fool me a bit. You figure you're any better than I am?"

Berutti fluttered his nostrils.

"The boys don't hang horses," he said. "Us stallions are too valuable for that—as long as mares are supposed to have foals, at least. It's just card thieves that get hung."

"*Hanged,*" I said. "*Hanged* is the proper form."

"Hung," Berutti insisted. And by the tone of his voice I knew the subject was closed.

Grouchy as he was being, I nevertheless went on tending to him. If I didn't do it, who was going to? I even found myself singing and whistling as I worked:

"In a cavern in a canyon
Excavating for a mine,
Dwelt a miner, Forty-Niner,
And his daughter, Clementine.

Oh my darling, oh my darling,
Oh my darling Clementine,
You are lost and gone forever,
Dreadful sorry, Clementine.

Light she was and like a fairy
And her shoes were number nine,
Herring boxes without topses
Sandals were for Clementine . . ."

I paused for a moment, listened carefully. The blue jays that had been shrieking were now quiet—quiet the way they get when something or someone is close at hand.

The stick's not floatin' right, Jesse. Mebbe you've got company.

Uncle Claude didn't talk to me all that often, but when he did, I listened. I hesitated for just an instant—and then turned quickly, my Colt-Patterson in hand, ready to kill a dozen men, just like always. But there was only the morning sun rimming the foothills off to the east—a flood of morning sunlight, and the callings of the blue jays once again. A jackrabbit made its way across the far side of the open meadow and stopped to wag his long ears, and then disappeared into some thickets of ceanothus and buckbrush beyond.

"Don't be so edgy, Jesse," I told myself—mimicking Uncle Claude's voice, or at least my memory of that voice.

I returned to work on Berutti, combing burrs out of

his mane. He, in turn, attempted once again to bite my arm, and I threatened to withhold both crackers and sweetening, two minor delicacies the stallion lived for.

Drove she ducklings to the water,
Ev'ry morning just at nine,
Hit her foot against a splinter,
Fell into the foaming brine.

Ruby lips above the water,
Blowing bubbles soft and fine,
Alas for me! I was no swimmer,
So I lost my Clementine.

In a churchyard, near the canyon,
Where the myrtle doth entwine,
There grow roses and other posies,
Fertilized by Clementine . . .

"You good singer for a fuck-king gringo. *Una canción popular . . .* So maybe I don't kill you after all. *Él que arqueda el caballo no arqueda la mujer.* Drop you gawddamn gun belt an' then turn around. I got you dead to right, Ace Tanner, an' now I take all your money, *todo.* Mebbe I just tie you up an' leave you to stew in your own juice, *te dejáran que rabies solo.* In a year or so someone probably find you—a skeleton wrapped in ropes. Only it is possible the wild dogs an' the possums, they eat the ropes too. Who knows? Or maybe you get loose before you starve to death, and in year or so we have another card game. If you yell loud enough, somebody come along an' set you free. Luck, she was with you in Mokelumne Hill—but now, Señor Tanner, *tienes mala suerte.* Your luck, it is gone very sour. Don' reach for the *pistola* or we kill you on the spot, eh, Juan José? Where's my Indio? She still alive? You have her long enough, gringo. Took her to the *médico* so she don't die, that's good, *bueno.* You save Jesus some money. For that I don't even cut off your *cojones.* I let you keep your life. Manzanita, is that her name? She comes with me. Where you hidin' *la chiflada*?

I calculated my chances. I might be able to squeeze off a shot or two before the Piedra bunch riddled me with lead, but both Piedra and his lanky companyero had their guns trained on me. I could go down gloriously or play for time, play the odds as I had always done before. A live dog, I concluded, would prove more worthy than a dead lion. In this case, of course, we were talking about a dead *gambolier*.

The glint in Jesus Piedra's eyes told me that he was hoping I might be rash enough to go for my pistol, him and Juan José having the drop on me and all. I grinned, shook my head.

"No point in calling," I said with a shrug. "This Yank folds. It's your hand, Jesus, my friend."

Slowly, deliberately, I unbuckled my holster and let my weapon fall to the ground. Piedra had seven men with him all told, and they looked like the kind that might wish to slit my throat at the least provocation. The tall one in particular had a glint in his eyes that I'd long since come to think of as the mark of the killer. For the moment, I was utterly at the mercy of the man I'd secretly vowed to kill. For his part, he could accomplish his purpose of retrieving both his money and his woman without ending up on a Wanted for Murder poster—though whether that possibility genuinely concerned him, I don't know.

"Out of tin, out of luck," I said. "It's your pot."

Piedra and his men took everything I had of any value—even Berutti the stallion and, of course, my Colt-Patterson with the notched handle, and bound me fast with strips of wet rawhide, lashed me to a scrub oak that was growing out from the base of a big, weathered granite boulder. He took my boots as well— on the off chance, I suppose, that I might actually manage to extricate myself. The chances of walking twenty miles without shoe leather were not good, but at the moment I wasn't particularly concerned about being without boots. After all, no man wants to die with his boots on, and that's especially true of gamblers.

"Good place for the *culebra*." Piedra laughed. "About the time you dying from thirst anyhow, the snake he'll come out and bite you on the *culo*. Then you swell and die, maybe faster. Or *permitido* somebody come along and help you to get loose, who knows? What's all the marks on the *pistola*? Are these hombres you kill in fair fights, or you tie 'em up first, then shoot 'em? Yankee target practice? Well, now you not even Catholic, but you get crucified anyhow. You gringos believe in *sagrado ascendiente*? Just tell your soul to fly right on out of its *cadáver*, Señor Tanner."

"Jesus, you must not leave him there," Manzanita protested, emerging from behind a screen of willow and alder that grew beside the creek. "I told you, he never touched me. Always you talk about honor. Show some honor! The gringo beat you at cards, and you let him win me. You should give him money—buy me back, like a man with *dignidad*."

"The leetle Indio, she talks too much, eh, Tanner? I show you how to deal with *la caída*."

To the general amusement of Piedra's men, he sent the Indian girl sprawling from a powerful backhanded blow that twisted her face around and left her bleeding from the nose and mouth. For a horribly long moment Manzanita lay in the brown grass, her long black hair thrown to one side of her face, unmoving, and I thought her neck might have been broken. But then she rolled over, used her good arm, winced noticeably, and got to her feet. She wiped the blood from her face and glared at Piedra.

"*Hijo de puta*," she said through clenched teeth. "Not even the vultures will wish to eat you."

"Indios, they never know what they saying. After a while maybe I tie her and whip her. You didn't even stick 'er, huh, gringo? Her skin the wrong color, or what? You afraid of her, or of me?"

"No man forgets his trade," I replied. "The rights of nations and of kings sink into questions of grammar if grammarians discuss them."

"*No comprendo*. Maybe you've gone crazy in the head, Tanner. You keep your fuck-king *pistola*. No damn good anyhow. You mark the cherry wood with lies."

With those words, Jesus Piedra mounted his horse, yanked Manzanita up behind him, and tossed my Colt-Patterson in the direction of the creek. Because of the way I was bound, I could not see where the weapon landed. If and when I was able to loose myself, I'd comb the area. That particular gun, I'd already decided, had at least one genuinely important job to do. Johnny Mankiller, he basically enjoyed his work.

I'll come find you, old friend, if I have the good fortune to get loose. Don't fall into a gopher hole. And avoid the rocks. A pistol with a bent barrel's no damned good at all.

How long it would take me to track Piedra, I didn't know, but track him I surely would.

"*Vaya con Díos, gringo!*" He laughed as he and his men rode away, with poor Berutti and Manzanita's mare, Deuce, trailing behind him. They could not have been more than a few hundred yards away when a shot was fired, then, in rapid succession, four more. My mind rebelled at the possible significance of the gunfire—I would not, could not, even think of it. Not until I'd managed to work my way loose.

The temperature had to be over a hundred—more than that, because I was bound there in direct sunlight, and the position of the sun indicated noon or something like that when I finally managed to wrench one hand free. The wet rawhide had shrunk about my wrists, naturally enough, and my hands were badly swollen. In rubbing my bonds back and forth over the rough bark of the little oak tree, I'd managed primarily to chafe and scour my own flesh. I presumed I was subject to gain a monumental infection, if the blinding San Joaquin Valley sun didn't dehydrate me into unconsciousness or cause my brain to explode within the skull.

When the wrist finally went numb, I doubled my efforts at abrading the rawhide. I could feel blood or perspiration or both dripping from my insensate fingertips, and in my mind's eye the bones of my wrist were certainly visible by this time.

Then the rawhide pulled loose, and for a moment I thought the sensation to be simply my imagination. The possibility of illusion was dispelled only when I brought my lacerated hand around from behind me. The fingers were almost black—dark blue from lack of circulation. I shook my hand back and forth, trying to regain feeling, and slowly a tingling, burning sensation began to emerge out of numbness. The feeling was far from pleasant, but under the circumstances, I found myself laughing out loud—though with a voice I could hardly recognize, for my tongue was also swollen and extremely dry. At least an hour earlier I had given up even trying to swallow.

I closed my eyes, hung my head, and attempted to gain strength through sheer resolve. Freeing myself completely was hardly a foregone conclusion, and some strange force within me had begun to suggest that I simply give up, try to sleep, let the summer sun have its way with me. I tried to imagine that someone on horseback would come by, some good Samaritan of a traveler who had strayed from the beaten track, or that Manzanita Huerfano herself might somehow have gotten away from Piedra and returned to rescue me.

For no good reason, the ideas of the philosopher Immanuel Kant, whose book I'd forced myself to read through a year earlier, came into my half-delirious mind. *Determine thyself from thyself.* What did the philosopher's assertion have to do with me and the potentially mortal predicament in which I found myself? I was at a point where I could barely discern what was me and what was the oak I was tied to. Was the meaning that of willing myself back toward life? Of escaping the boundaries of my rapidly weakening physical body? Or of taking my present self, not worth much at all given the circumstances, and distinguishing my spiritual being as distinct from the physical—or of creating a new self out of the ashes and ruins of the old?

Tanner, ye stupid dumb sonofabitch, get to working on those thongs while ye're still able to do 'er. A few more hours o' this sunlight, and you're not subject to be much of anything. Take note of them two, three turkey vultures swingin' around up thar. They're looking you over, Ace, my boy.

A little burst of wind poured around me, and that was when I realized just how serious my situation was. I could feel almost no cooling sensation, and that in turn meant no perspiration on my face at all. If I squinted or even tried to grin, I was aware of a dull pain.

Above the rim to the east, but very far away, were great towers of cumulus, thunderheads, rank upon rank of them building their huge cathedrals in the sky above the distant Sierra Nevada. If only those clouds would drift my way, would bring me rain. . . .

My fingers were still essentially without sensation, and not being able to see the bindings that held me behind my back, I could do little more than struggle and try to curse—but my tongue was so thick I couldn't even do that. I could manage little more than to moan and squeak.

The image of Jesus Piedra tied to a similar tree, and me standing there in front of him, laughing, laughing—that vision gave me heart, and eventually I was able to free my other hand.

Even then, it was all I could do to work at the knots that held me fast. At length I managed to push a wide band of green leather from my chest to my mouth, and then I commenced to chewing. Saliva formed in my mouth, thank God, and I could swallow once more, although painfully. But I chewed through the leather and eventually, with thanks to the powers above, I unwrapped myself. When I could finally sit at the foot of the little oak, I was fortunate enough to find an egg-sized chunk of jagged rock, and with this I managed to saw through the worn-out length of lariat that had been used to bind my ankles.

Stumbling, crawling, then rising to my feet once again, hardly even aware of being without my boots, buoyed by an infinite sense of outrage, I made my way to the creek, lay fully in the shallow water and forced myself to do no more than to sip, holding the water in my mouth for a long while before swallowing.

Without strength to rise to my feet, I turned onto my back and allowed the slack current to tickle its way about me. I squinted at the crowns of the creek alders and admired the way the sunlight, almost as though it were some strange and melodic variety of green music, almost like the ancient panpipe itself, worked its way among the leaves and filtered to where I lay in the stream.

"Lord," I whispered, "I know I ought to thank you for letting me get free. But goddamn it, why'd you have to let that *cholo* tie me up in the first place? It's got to be just blind bad luck that he stumbled onto our campsite—unless maybe someone in Mokelumne Hill told him or one of his riders where it was I was planning to go, which road I took. You're not the one who pointed him the way, are you? If you keep treating me like this, God, old friend, what makes you think I'm ever going to put a dollar in your donation plate again? Use logic, damn it. Didn't anyone ever tell you that honey works better than vinegar if you're trying to trap flies?"

Tanner, you're babbling. Turn over, drink some more water, and then look for your pistol. You're not dead yet, and that means you're obliged to survive. And that

*also means you've got to find your pistol or get an-
other one and another horse as well. The stash you put
in the bank in Mokelumne Hill, that was good thinking. I suppose there's at least a little hope for you.*

"Sonofabitch," I said as I did what I was told.

*True enough. When you're ready, climb the ledge
and check around those ferns. Piedra tossed the
damned thing over there somewhere. . . .*

Once I had my wits more or less about me again,
and once I'd taken in enough water to float Noah's
Ark, I stumbled my way downstream, in the direction
Piedra and his party had taken, all the while dreading
what I might come upon—namely, Manzanita's body,
dried blood all over her, flies already laying their
cursed eggs in the red blossoms of her mortal wounds,
in her mouth, in her eyes. . . .

But there was no body—no sign of anything of the
sort. I followed the hoof marks for perhaps half a mile,
cursing because of my tender and now bruised feet,
and found nothing unusual at all. My mind somewhat
at ease by now, I limped my way back to the site of my
crucifixion, as Piedra called it, determined to find Sir
Jonathan Mankiller. Without boots, I could get along
for a time. I could even manage without having Berutti
to talk to. But I had to have that pistol. Piedra's mark
hadn't been carved on it yet.

Later that afternoon I did indeed find Johnny the
Colt-Patterson—stuck barrel first in some mud near a
spot where numerous clumps of fern were growing,
just as the voice had told me. Truth to say, I'd been listening to that voice off and on for years, and sometimes it was actually helpful. Maybe it was my own
voice, but the voice I would have when I was fifty or
sixty. You suppose that's possible? I mean, that we
carry around inside of us not only the kids we used to
be, but the worn-out guys we're going to be—if we're
lucky enough to get there, I mean.

I also found the remnant of the side of bacon I'd put

in the fork of an alder, away from our sleeping robes, and high enough so that a damned griz or black bear couldn't easily get at it. That is to say, I found the bacon all right, but it wasn't there where I left it. Instead the slab was at shoulder height, stuck back in between the fronds of a wild lilac bush.

Only one explanation was possible. Manzanita must have put the meat there, hoping I'd free myself and knowing that I'd need something to eat, and that bacon was sure as the devil better than nothing at all.

Amazingly enough, a trickle of smoke was now rising from the fire pit I'd utilized the previous night, even though nothing had been evident in the immediate aftermath of my freeing myself. I took note of this stroke of good fortune and quickly gathered handfuls of dry grass, placed these carefully above where the trace of smoke issued, and blew softly. At first just ashes swirled up, giving me a snootful, but then the grass began to burn, and I quickly scrambled about to fetch twigs and curlings of alder bark.

In no time I had a respectable little blaze going, and, lacking even a knife, I placed the entire chunk of bacon between two wrist-thick branches and waited for the meat to sizzle awhile. After everything that had already happened, I reflected, I surely didn't want to die because some little hairlike worms had worked their way into my liver and brain—or whatever the hell it is they do, though to tell the truth, I've always rather enjoyed an occasional piece of raw pork, cured or not.

Besides, a gambler's supposed to die either with a bullet in his back or at the end of a good strong hemp.

So this time I decided to play it safe.

When I explored among the alders for additional firewood—squaw wood, as the boys called it then—I found my Bowie knife, still in its leather scabbard, standing against a tree trunk, right where she must have left it for me to find.

"Manzanita, little Manzanita. . . . This was all you could do for me, but it's enough. I'll pull through for sure, and I'll come find you too. I swear it. I'll come find you, young lady, whether you want me to or not. When Ace Tanner sets his mind to a thing, it's as good as *done*, I'll tell ye."

Six

BAPTISM WITH THUNDER

As he was driving down one night,
As lively as a coon,
He saw four men jump in the road
By the pale light of the moon.

One sprung for his leaders,
While another his gun he cocks,
Saying, "My fellow, I hate to trouble you,
But pass me out that box!"

When the driver heard him say these words,
He opened wide his eyes,
He didn't know what in the world to do,
It took him by surprise.

But he reached down into the boot,
Saying, "Take it, sir, with pleasure,"
And out into the middle of the road
Went Wells & Fargo's treasure.

They played four hands against his one,
And shotguns was their game,
And if I'd been in that driver's place,
I'd have passed the box the same.

First I heard some noise in the brush. Since I was still in the process of using a willow twig and a scrap of cloth to get the mud out of Johnny Mankiller's barrel, the pistol obviously wasn't going to do me any good at all. You get mud in your barrel, and pistol or rifle, either one, will blow up in your face. Something like that could disfigure a fellow, permanent, you understand. So I grabbed the Bowie knife and scrambled off to a hiding place behind a couple of downed alders next to the creek. Whoever had come to visit was by-God not going to take me by surprise.

Piedra?

If it was him, come back to finish the job, the *cholo* was by himself. There was no way half a dozen green'uns could sneak up on Ace Tanner, not all in a bunch. Well, I guess that wasn't quite true. Jesus and his gang, after all, had taken me by surprise just recently.

This time, I mused, I'd hack somebody's leg off at the very least.

Then a long, beady-eyed equine head thrust out from among some gray-green ceanothus brush.

"Good afternoon, boss."

I broke out laughing.

"Berutti? How in hell did you get loose? Ain't nobody following you, is there?"

The stallion shook his head and fluttered his lips.

"Heck no. When this horse decides to make a break for freedom, he takes a few shortcuts, if you know what I mean. Don Juan Piedra's thieves were talking about turning me into an equine roast, and that's not the kind of *payasadas* that appeals to me. I figured it was time to put some distance between me and them. A couple of hills, a couple of gullies. And of course I don't dawdle. Fellows like Jesus and his thieving friends, they get frustrated, and after that they turn real ugly. Me, I stick to the brush, cross over a ridge, get out of their line of fire. A bad-natured stallion like myself, you know, that's nothing to them. Hell, they'd shoot me just to get your fancy saddle back. For all I know, they'd shoot me for the bloody fun of it. Well, mate, am I wrong or not?"

I could tell by Berutti's expression that he was at least passingly concerned about my standing there, waving the Bowie knife about. The idea of someone carving on his vitals clearly did not appeal to him. Noting the momentary confusion, I thrust the blade into the ground and leaped toward the wild lilacs behind which my faithful companyero and mode of transport was standing. I hugged him, and he, as if to return the favor, nipped at my hair.

"You weren't thinking about taking that damn dagger to me, were you, boss? I came back, didn't I? I didn't make you come look for me on foot. Act civilized, damn it."

"Right you are, old friend," I said. "The knife's the only weapon I had at the moment. For all I knew, you realize, Piedra himself was. . . . Aw hell, Berutti, you know me better than that. But right now I'm thinking that it's about time for you and me both to change our ways. There's got to be a safer method of making a living. As for myself, I think I may just have been falling in love with a certain little señorita."

"You're saying a gambler's got no business dragging a wife around behind him? Right?"

"Precisely my thought."

Berutti, he began chewing on the ceanothus branches, and I could tell he was done talking for a time. He didn't want me to bring up the issue of Manzanita's little gray mare, Deuce. We both knew he was soft on her, and only genuine loyalty had brought him back to me. There's nothing better than having a good horse—it's the kind of bond, I mean, that precious few humans can understand.

Well, not many things better, at least.

• • •

"The way I see it, Dr. Berutti," I said to my faithful stallion, "we might just be in real luck. You've still got your saddlebags on, and in the bottom here we should find a handful of ammunition all tied up in a *lit-tle* canvas bag. Money we don't need, not right at the moment at least. But ammo we've got a definite use for. . . ."

Berutti said nothing, and I got the feeling that he was done talking for a while. He was kind of like that horse in *The Iliad*, you might say, only Berutti didn't require any gods or goddesses to make him turn conversational. It had occurred to me once or twice that he'd have made a hell of a carnival horse—except, unfortunately, the fact that I was the only one he ever talked to, and he didn't talk to me very damned often.

The caps, powder, and lead were right where I hoped they'd be. In a matter of no time I'd be on my way. Piedra's victim was about to turn into a hunting bird, a condor, you might say, but one with real talons.

Vengeance is mine, saith Uncle Claude.

Within an hour we were on the trail, downstream along Cosgrove's Creek to where it emptied into the Calaveras River, the river of skulls. Piedra's trail was easy enough to follow, in point of fact, since a dozen horses are bound to leave their marks as well as their droppings, and the way Piedra's bunch were heading wasn't followed by very many. I've always thought it an irony that highwaymen spend less time on highways than virtually anyone else, since they're generally not looking for company. They touch a main trail, lay in wait for a likely victim, tend to their business, and then disappear into the chaparral again.

At the river, they'd turned southwest as the stream led, out into the grasslands of the San Joaquin Valley. Heading for the town of Stockton? The little river swung westward, and not too many miles of barren grassland and range would bring me to what was, in those days, one of California's chief cities—right there along with Marysville, Grass Valley, Sacramento, San Francisco, and Monterey.

But then the trail veered south by southeast, toward Littlejohn's Creek and Lone Tree. By the time the sun was ready to drop behind the Coast Range way off across the big valley, I was heading into new territory. The map I carried in my skull would need some filling in, but that was all right with me.

When would I catch up? Why, then I'd have the minor problem of dealing not merely with Jesus Piedra, but also with his companyeros. And if indeed I could pull off that minor miracle, would the lovely Manzanita Huerfano come with me, a drifting card thief who was in most ways not a damned bit better than the murdering cur she was cursed with at present?

At the very least, then, I could kill Piedra and thus set Manzanita free. Hell, she already knew she was free, a free woman and a grandfathered-in, by-Gawd citizen of the Republic, an American citizen. So why was she still hanging around with that dung-eating dog?

Well, maybe she liked dogs—and that was the significance of her coyote medallion. Coyote the wise one, coyote the thief in the night, consumer of chickens and unattended sides of venison and the like.

I thought about one coyote that I caught red-pawed, so to speak, not far from Taos. I'd stashed my grub and had gone out after setting up camp—had ridden out to pop a couple of jackrabbits or possibly a javelina or whatever came my way. Well, I returned empty-handed, and there was Uncle Coyote, nose into my last bag of flour. Gave him a white beard, so to speak. He looked so damned ridiculous, partly for the flour all over him and partly for getting surprised that way, that he just stood there waiting for me to shoot him. But I didn't, of course, because it was all plain comical, and I burst out laughing and couldn't have aimed Johnny

Mankiller even if I'd wanted to. I tipped my hat to *Señor Coyotl*, and we called it a draw.

I grinned at the memory, watched the great orange-red ellipse of the sun drop into the Coast Range far to the west, and kept on riding.

The way I figured things, Jesus Piedra had been fairly confident that I was never going to get away from that tree he tied me to. Nobody was likely to be stopping by, not a mile or so from the trail that way, not unless some prospector happened along and took pity on me. Most likely I'd just shrivel in the sun, and by the time someone did find me, I'd be made out of leather—except that the woods rats and the possums and the vultures would have worked me over pretty good. Maybe the discoverers of my grotesque remains would have cut me loose and hauled me back to Mokelumne Hill for some kind of bizarre Halloween decoration.

"Berutti," I said, rubbing him under the mane, "tell me again how it happened that you got loose. There's something peculiar as the devil in all this."

But Berutti wasn't in a mood to answer.

Would Piedra have turned back? Would he have made any attempt at all to track down the jail-breaking stallion? The horse, in a land where the ranchos had hundreds out on the range and no one to protect the animals from the occasional *ladrón de caballos*, was not so valuable an animal that great time would be spent tracking a particular pony, though with a fancy saddle and trappings, perhaps that would be a different matter. Berutti might well have been deemed valuable more for what he was wearing than for what he actually was.

It occurred to me that I could very well have had a few of Piedra's men behind me somewhere back in the gathering darkness and a few others ahead of me but coming back along the very trail I was following—though this scenario wasn't all that likely, I had to admit. Chances were that Piedra and his band were twenty miles ahead of me, happily settled in for the night, with a big cooking fire already started and a haunch of venison or antelope or possibly beef from a not-sufficiently-wary range cow. And perhaps Manzanita, bandaged side and all, would be running her fingers across the strings of her guitar and singing in the Spanish of Old California and the days of Micheltorena and Pío Pico.

If all that were so, was she also thinking (at least momentarily) about the Yankee card thief who had won her at a game of chance? A Yank who had offered her the proper gift of freedom, when indeed freedom was already hers?

Berutti sampled the twilight air and whinnied. Strangely enough, a great horned owl replied—the easily identified *who, who, whoo-whoo-whoo* echoing through the darkness and the odors of dry grass and thistle and the foliage of water oaks and madronas.

Possibly the big guy just wanted his evening dole of grain. Fortunately Piedra and his thieves hadn't ransacked my saddlebags at all—and indeed, that rather suggested the good Dr. Berutti hadn't been held in captivity very long. The criminal's instinct would have taken Jesus and his compadres at least a couple of miles before they'd have worried about small change such as might have been in the saddlebags of a newly pilfered horse. A quick search would have told them I wasn't carrying any appreciable amount of money, and Manzanita must have provided the explanation.

"If you want it, Jesus, you'll have to rob a bank to get it." I laughed.

Of course, I too might well be obliged to return to Mokelumne Hill in order to avail myself of my funds—though possibly in Coarse Gold, where I'd heard that my cousin Jamie Savage was running a mercantile and was, of all things unlikely, an honest-to-God *major* in a volunteer militia known as the Mariposa Battalion, I'd be able to present my letters of credit until such time as funds could be transferred from one bank to the other.

Urging Berutti ahead, I rode on into the darkness, ever wary, picking my way until I could no longer see to pick at all. By means of full utilization of the least remnant of twilight, I figured I'd be able to gain a few miles and thus cut the distance between us. I realized I was taking a chance, but under the circumstances, I guessed the odds were on my side. I'd eat cold, somewhat burned bacon and ride again with first light. Berutti grumbled, but we found a swampy area with abundant grass. The hour was well after sundown, and fortunately the damnable valley mosquitoes were dining elsewhere—or clinging to oak leaf or willow stem or whatever it is that they do when they're not tormenting horses and humans. If the new state of California ever had need of an official state bird, it would be a toss-up between the condor and the valley mosquito.

After the heat of afternoon, night was remarkably cool. Only a few stars were visible now, and I suspected there might even be a shower before morning. Those huge towers of cloud that had hung far eastward during the day, noticeable even as I was being crucified on the goddamn oak and half dead of dehydration, over the backs of the Sierra Nevada—*Mount Joseph*, as Jed Smith had once called the mountains whose snows had so effectively acted as a barrier against the rest of the continent—sometimes drifted westward and doused the valley floor. And when that happened, it was damned pleasant.

I mean the showers, not getting crucified. Truth to tell, I made a damned bad show of being a Christ figure, though I had personally put Lazarus to bed a few times and often told the devil where to stand.

Off in the distance: thunder rolling high over the range, the waves of noise muted but still recognizable after a fellow considered matters for a moment or two. Thor and Loki, it occurred to me, were shouting at one another—and no telling who was winning the argument. Perhaps, as I thought the matter through, they were discussing the fate of one Jesse Ace Tanner, but behind his back. Isn't that always the way of things, by God?

Just then, the very moment I was thinking about how good a downpour would be, that strange hush came over the land, and big, big drops of rain began to fall. I led Berutti back under the cover of a monstrous live oak, and I pulled off my saddle, saddlebags, and blanket, and left my faithful stallion to his own devices. I could tell that he wanted to wander over to the edge of the swampy area, but he didn't like the idea of getting wet.

Thus we spent the rainy night together, me with a horse blanket for cover and a saddle for a pillow, and the good doctor, annoyed by the damp turn of events, stamping from side to side and chewing pathetically at the rough bark of the big live oak.

"Go to sleep, you sonofabitch," I said after a time, but Berutti, he didn't answer. Not in so many words, at least.

Just as I had gotten comfortable and was drifting away into sleep and possibly into dreams as well, lighting struck close by. My eyes were open at the very instant, and what I saw was hard to believe—a digger pine coiled in a great vine of electricity not more than a hundred yards distant, just across the way from where Berutti and I had taken shelter. Then the light was gone, and darkness was gorged with overwhelming noise. A few pinecones must have dislodged—or limbs broken away. In any case, I could hear things falling—falling and striking other limbs on the way down. And the rich smell of crushed foliage was on the air. I was aware of the odors, however, only in the aftermath. In the present moment one could hardly have been aware of anything other than the earthquakelike heaves of noise, there was so much of it.

Berutti shrieked and tried to get closer to me. Had it

not been for the big live oak we were under, the damned fool horse would have stepped right on top of me.

A baptism of fire and tides of noise and spates of summer rain . . .

Because rain was indeed falling, falling as though God's many wounds had chosen to spill themselves all at once into the darkness of the summer night.

With first light I was back on Piedra's trail, a trail easily followed. The big valley, broad between mountain ranges to the east and the west, stretched on endlessly, undulating grasslands that sometimes gave way to sage and greasewood and thistle, with oasislike glades of oak and alder along the rivers that had worked their way from the mysterious hinterland of the Sierra, the vast *Inyo*, as I'd heard a couple of Indian friends call it.

Piedra and his gang scrupulously avoided all settlements, but at length the trail crossed what I presumed to be the fledgling San Joaquin River, one of its southernmost branches, at least, and then turned southwest toward the emergent cow town of Fresno.

I went first to a newly opened branch of the Wells & Fargo and, with a great deal of difficulty, was able to discount some bills of credit at the rate of forty percent. The banker knew he had me at a disadvantage, and I knew it as well. Never bet when the other guy's got a pair of aces showing, that's what I say. In any case, money's like the wind, and I had ways of restoring my stash, or so I supposed. Under the circumstances, after all, I was lucky as hell to be able to pull off such an exchange, even if I was cheated. It was pure luck that Piedra hadn't searched my person more thoroughly—and that no one had thought to get into Berutti's saddlebags right away, as I've noted previously.

With help from the bank, then, I was able to restore my remuda. That is, I bought a new mule to haul my outfit along—stuff that I proceeded to acquire at the Long Horn Mercantile & Leather Company. With supplies, lariat, ammunition, a used Sharps rifle in mediocre shape, some blankets, and the like, I made my way to the first of three tavernas. Fresno prices were high, at least to strangers, and the grubstake fairly well exhausted my new wad.

No Piedra. No Manzanita. But there was a game of blackjack that I couldn't resist. Hell, I needed to get my financial affairs back into shape, didn't I?

Within a couple of hours I was just over two hundred dollars richer, mostly in fines and nuggets, but some in old Californio silver as well. I ordered drinks all around, thanked the lads sincerely, and proceeded on my mission.

At the third of the tavernas, I elicited some significant information about Jesus Piedra. He and half a dozen of his men had been there that morning and proceeded to get soused. Yet no one had seen anything of a certain strangely beautiful Indian girl. I nodded, paid for a drink of my own, tossed it off, and then resisted the temptation to participate in a session of seven-card stud.

I walked back out into the oppressive heat of the afternoon, watered Berutti and the mule, and set off southward along the main street of Fresno. I knew now, or had strong suspicions, where friend Piedra was headed, for the bartender had given me that tittle of information. Jesus Piedra, as it turned out, was relatively notorious. He had, I learned, a village hidden back in the Tehachapi Mountains to the west of Tejon Pass— near the peak called Piños, Pine Mountain. The place was called, poetically enough, the Fortress, a place where even the *alcaldes* thought it best not to venture.

I was able to pick up the trail once again, heading due south now. I pushed ahead at a good pace, despite the blinding heat of the San Joaquin Valley and Berutti's grouching, but I was still unable to overtake my quarry. That night I camped alongside the Río de los Santos Reyes, Kings River, which was said to rise somewhere back in the formidable Sierra to the east, among the highest of the peaks.

I made a fire, a small one so as not to attract unwanted attention, and roasted some hanging tenderloins that I'd purchased in Fresno. Though the meat had been in good shape just a few hours earlier, and though the butcher had double-wrapped it in waxed paper and green steer hide, the heat of afternoon had half charred it—dried and crusted the surface. Nonetheless, the fresh beef tasted damned good—the first I'd enjoyed in several days.

Berutti savored his corn, oats, and barley and thereafter lay on his side, sprawled out like a dead horse, and began to snore loudly.

"Damn it," I muttered, half to myself and half to my sleeping stallion. "They can't be far ahead of me. I've been pushing hard. But maybe they're running from something—or toward something. . . ."

I was too tired to pursue the matter any further than that. Tomorrow would come soon enough. One way or another, I'd sure as hell catch up with them.

Piedra and his gang of thieves had now resorted to the main route south toward the Tejon Pass—not a road, you understand, or anything of the sort. Rather, this was the venue commonly taken by cattle drovers through a broad, desolate region. Horses from the north were often herded south to the vicinity of the Los Angeles Pueblo and exchanged for tough, trailworthy Spanish cattle that might in turn then be driven back north to the mining regions, where beef sold at an absolute premium and where the market for leather and so forth was top dollar. Men who were wild with lust for yellow metal weren't much concerned about raising meat animals—or in growing corn or potatoes, for that matter, or in doing anything else but *mining*—as though obsessed with the idea of digging themselves back into the earth into which they'd be lowered in due course, I reflected, whether they dug or not. The ranchos of the northern San Joaquin and the Sacramento, already in existence at the time of the beginning of the Rush, were simply not sufficient to produce what was needed. So long as gold was plentiful and prices high, there would be those who undertook to supply meat, potatoes, clothing, tools, and so on. In the same way, there would always be opportunities aplenty for men like myself, individuals who lived and died on the turn of a card. Farmers, merchants, blacksmiths, and gamblers all lived on the backs of miners who worked up to their asses in cold, muddy water, and who possessed no talent at all for hanging on to the tin they garnered by means of their labors.

As to why anyone should wish to avail himself of gold, that was another matter. Indians called the stuff *worthless yellow metal*, since unlike iron or bronze, for instance, it had no intrinsic utilitarian value.

And all of this is true, but commerce isn't what concerned me. What I made note of was that a considerable herd of cattle had recently been driven northward, and Piedra's trail, so easily discernible when it ran across empty grasslands, was now increasingly difficult to detect.

When I reached Tule River, I ran out of sign. Cattle had apparently been driven downstream from a hacienda somewhere upriver, perhaps from the grasslands at the foot of the Sierra. The main trail lay ahead of me, but telltale marks of Piedra's remuda were no longer visible.

Even without reason to believe he was being trailed, and certainly not by Ace Tanner (who ought to have been dead at that point), had the cunning of the highwayman dictated that the gang separate, to reunite at some point closer to their little kingdom high in the Tehachapis? Or had Jesus Piedra sent his men off on some "errand"?

At a likely spot on the trail, an interval of powdery clay that had been turned to thin mud during a recent thunder shower such as the one I myself had experienced a few days earlier, I dismounted and examined the scattering of horse tracks temporarily preserved by the heat of the sun. There was sign, all right, three horses so far as I could tell, but all of them large-hoofed. No sign of Deuce.

Berutti chewed halfheartedly at a clump of wheat grass that was not entirely brown with the late summer. Then he pursed his lips and spat it out.

"Wrong flavor?" I asked.

"All bones and no meat," he replied. "Boss, you don't suppose Manzanita's riding a different *caballo* now, do you? As for the mare, little Deuce, hell, she turned off to the east way back there. That's why I was snorting and spitting three or four hours ago."

"That so?" I said. "Then why in hell didn't you say something, you damned fool? Why the devil do you think we came clear down here, halfway to the end of the known world? That was our purpose—to catch up with Manzanita—and your friend Deuce."

"The mare had possibilities, I'll admit it. But as for saying something, Mr. Tanner, you know in your heart that I'm just a horse, and horses don't talk. Besides, you were the one in the saddle. Reverse our roles, I'll tell you, and we'd see better results. . . ."

The good doctor had a point.

Piedra might well have given Manzanita a different pony. For that matter, he might well have traded her to one of his cohorts for some favor or another—Deuce or Manzanita, either one. The fact was, I'd lost the certain trail I'd been following, and now I was going to have to backtrack—or be guided by my instincts and keep heading for Tejon country. I'd meet someone, without doubt, who could direct me to the general vicinity of Piedra's hideout. There's always someone who knows of Piedra's whereabouts, if you get my drift.

Seven

BECKWOURTH & THE GHOST OF McCOOL

You're looking now at Jesse Ace Tanner,
A relic of bygone days;
A bummer, too, they call me so,
But what care I for praise?

My heart is filled with the days of yore,
And oft I do repine
For the Days of Old, and the Days of Gold,
And the Days of 'Forty-Nine.

I had some pals who loved me well,
And a horse that was faithful and true;
There were some hard cases, I must confess,
Who liked all the lead and the hullabaloo;

Who would never flinch, what'er the pinch,
And never would fret or whine,
But like good old bricks they stood the kicks
In the Days of 'Forty-Nine.

There was Monté Claude—I'll ne'er forget
The luck he always had,
He would deal for you both day and night,
As long as you had a scad.

He would play you draw, he would ante sling,
He would go you a hatful blind—

But in a game of Death Claude lost his breath
In the Days of 'Forty-Nine.

After following several trails that led me nowhere I wanted to go, I turned southward once
again, and as the heat of the day diminished
toward nightfall, I found myself in proximity to a
wide and doubtless shallow lake far out near the center of the Big Valley—no surprise, actually, for the
boys in Fresno had mentioned the fact that Lake
Tulare was full again this year after two or three
seasons of low water, at least according to the Californio vaqueros, since in point of fact there had been
no Yanks about at that time to make proper witness
of the extent of the lake. It was a body of water
the old-timers—those who'd been around five or
six months—insisted that sometimes filled half the
valley and sometimes shrank away to nothing. The
first Spanish to cross the Tehachapis, so the story
went, looked on what they supposed must be an arm
of the ocean, so extensive had been Tulare at that
time.

What I could see for myself was that there was
no shoreline ring of trees, such as one might have
expected, this peculiarity owing most likely to the
extreme seasonality of the lake. Only on truly excep-
tional years would the water overflow and make its
way northward to confluence with the Kings River or
the San Joaquin.

But I also observed something else.

There was smoke from a campfire, barely visible
as the western sky went bloodred above the Coast
Ranges, nearly fifty miles distant as I guessed. *A single
fire.* This would not, then, be Piedra and his gang,
though if Jesus and Manzanita had taken to riding

alone, with the remainder of the gang on their own separate trek southward toward Piños . . .

I urged Berutti ahead and made my way cautiously toward the smoke. As twilight gathered I observed the group—perhaps a dozen in all, and clearly not Piedra nor any of his gang of thieves.

In the time-honored way of the mountains, I fired Johnny Mankiller twice into the sky and proceeded at an easy walk into the camp area. I was, I thought, ready for nearly anything, but I must admit that what followed was an utter surprise.

Two or three Americans and a number of Indians were eating dinner and listening to none other than Jim Beckwourth himself tell one of his famous tall tales—though if Jim had been telling the Lord's truth, that wouldn't have changed things a bit. As I think I mentioned earlier, Beckwourth was perhaps fifty at the time, not really so old, as these things go—an extremely impressive figure of a man, though it's always difficult to see in a mere human being the embodied legend of one of those giants of the opening of the Rocky Mountains. Same with Bridger and Meek and Carson and O'Bragh. At first glance you'd swear they were just plain human beings, like the rest of us. Indeed, at first I didn't realize the identity of the tall, rangy storyteller, even though I'd met him before and spent some time talking with him. Only when Jim called out to me did I realize who he was.

"Come on in, young fellow, and share the meat bag with us. Ace Tanner, is that you? Well by God, welcome, welcome. Good to see ye again. These boys are my friends—no harm in the bunch of them. Not a bad thought in any of their skulls, sure enough, and you have my word on it! Not a child among us has killed anyone all day long."

"As long as they're of a mind to keep the string going," I replied, "I'll be pleased to have your company. My name's Tanner, gents."

"Famous gambler," Beckwourth explained to his

companyeros. "Once lost his skulp to a Pawnee over at Rendezvous, but by God the next year he won 'er back again. A brush full o' tar to put it in place, and he was good as ever. Show the boys yore ha'r, Ace," Jim said, looking as serious as death itself.

I dismounted, assessing the situation as I did so, and then, having tied Berutti short—in case I should have to get back to him quickly—I strode casually to the circle of firelight.

Beckwourth had the unique quality of being able to dominate, center stage, whatever group he happened to be in. So commanding was his presence that at first I hardly noticed the old salt seated beside him, a much shorter man and thickly bearded, the hair white, but his pate itself bald as the summit of Shasta, yet decorated, so to speak, with a jagged scar—as though someone had indeed tried to scalp him but had botched the job. This individual suddenly stood—as though he'd seen a ghost.

The beard was different, but a man can carry his chin whiskers in any one of a dozen fashions, and scars come from the simple fact of living. . . . Something damnably familiar about . . .

"Jesse Tanner, lad, is that you? For God's sake, man, say something. I thought I'd seen the last o' ye for sure. . . ."

Nail my twenty-dollar boots to the ground, it can't be, it's not goddamn possible, is it?

"Claude McCool?" I blurted out. "Stranger, I could almost swear . . ."

"O' course it's Claude McCool, Jesse. Have ye gone blind or what? What in God's name are ye doin' out hyar in California? It's me, your own uncle Claude. If I didn't know better, I'd swear ye look like Mike McLafferty hisself. . . ."

"It is—you? Goddamnit, Claude, you're dead, murdered in St. Louis and thrown into the river and—"

"Well, ye damned fool, are ye goin' to believe your own eyes, or what? Nobody murders Claude McCool an' gets away with it. Ain't my nature to let no one take advantage of me thataway."

"He's not dead, Ace, and I'll testify to it in a court of law," Beckwourth said, straight-faced. "A little slow, but definitely not dead. You two know each other, as I take it?"

Then Claude and I were pounding one another on the back, and it was as if we had just seen each other last a few hours ago, back in St. Louis—though indeed nearly fifteen years had elapsed. As the Bible insisted, of course, Lazarus returned from the dead, though he had some powerful help, a friend in high places. That Uncle Claude McCool should reappear, on the other hand, and after so long a time, was simply an outrageous reversal of fate. Not even in one of those dime novels could such a thing happen.

Except for the beard and the dome a little more barren than before, McCool didn't even seem to have changed all that much—though surely he was in his mid-seventies by this time, ancient enough to have been a father to Jim Beckwourth himself.

"Jim," Claude laughed, "this'n was jest a boy when I kidnapped him, so to speak, and took him west to St. Louis, your hometown. I tried to settle down back in Pennsylvania, ye see, but all the ladies had tight asses.... Anyhow, we set up operations in St. Louis, an' Jesse hyar took to playin' cards. Guess we sort of lost track of each other for a spell...."

Beckwourth and his Indian friends had by now closed around the two of us, perhaps wondering whether we'd recall some ancient grudges and take to murdering one another.

"Tanner, is this the coot who taught ye the magic of cards? I've heard that you're fast with a horse pistol too, and cool as any cucumber at the playing table."

"Rumor," I told Beckwourth, "mere rumor. If I know anything about cards at all, then I learned it from this reprobate right here."

"True enough!" McCool cackled. "Set down, lad. Ye

must be starvin'. Jimmy hyar, he shot us a proper tule elk this afternoon, an' we was jest samplin' the hindquarters. Hell, I'll fetch my canteen full o' whiskey, an' we'll all have a snort."

I sat next to the campfire, and Jim Beckwourth himself cut me a big chunk of elk flesh. It was hot and good and greasy, I'll tell you, and I couldn't think when anything tasted a whole lot better.

When we finally finished talking and had bedded down for the night, I reflected on the astonishing significance of what had just, by chance as it were, occurred. Claude, whom I assumed to be dead lo these many years, was actually still alive and kicking—and, as I gathered, had just come back into my life in a more or less permanent way. *Permanent*, however, was a human term, and God was in no way obliged to honor it.

I could detect Claude's snoring above the snores of all the others, Beckwourth and his Indian friends, and there was something reassuring about the sound. Somewhere north along the lakeshore, however temporary that may have been, I could hear a band of coyotes yapping their heads off. That sound, too, was damnably reassuring, for it seemed, inexplicably, to stress the moral order inherent within our otherwise utterly random world.

I thought of Manzanita Huerfano's little silver and turquoise coyote medallion, and I wondered if the young woman had indeed thought about me even once since that morning when Piedra tied me to the tree.

She must of been thinking of ye, otherwise she wouldn't've set Berutti loose....

If that was what had happened.

The coyotes continued to howl, and I imagined two of them there, heads tilted back, mouth-to-mouth, ululating for all the world to hear.

After a breakfast of bad coffee and cold elk venison, Claude and I departed together. Beckwourth was headed north in any case, and as matters turned out, he and McCool had met one another on the trail, and so Claude had strung along, even though Jim and his Indian friends were headed north, to Hangtown, where he and Pompey Charbonneau had built a tavern and rooming house—Charbonneau having given up on trapping a few years earlier and having wound up in California, just as so many of us coons had done. In truth, Claude's original destination had been San Diego. Now he was headed south once again, with me, astraddle a white mule he called Optimist, Oppy for short, because she was prone to look at the bright side of matters.

Claude and I rode together for a spell, talking our fool heads off. I mean, when your mentor comes back from the dead, and after so long a time, you've got some catching up to do, both of you. But there's no sense in repeating everything we said, especially what I said, since I've already told you most of that. As for Claude, to hear him tell it, he was little more than a bag full of infirmities of one sort or another, "the gen'ral curse o' getting old," which was the same phrase he was fond of when I knew him years earlier. As I say, from my point of view, Uncle Claude seemed hardly to have changed at all, except in minor ways.

Naturally, however, in more than a decade, numerous things were bound to have happened. The Kaw Indians had cut off three of Claude's fingers as a punishment for cheating at cards, and the Rees, a few years later, had left him for dead, half scalped. That incident was the cause of the vivid scar that stood out on Claude's bald head. Why the Rees didn't finish the job, I don't know, and I never asked. Some things, I guess, need to remain personal.

From the awkwardness of some of his motions, I surmised that arthritis did indeed bedevil him at times, just as he said.

"O' course I heard about Ace Tanner, all right," Claude said, "an' once or twice I wondered if it might be you. Rumor had it you was plyin' your trade in Stumptown, Oregon. Otherwise, I might of looked ye up. Met a fella from Oregon country just a couple of weeks back, as it turns out, an' he said he was hunting for a gambler by the name o' Ace—fella about your age, name of Billingwood, I believe it were. If it's you he was lookin' for, he ain't no friend. Says he has a score to settle, at cards or otherwise."

"Abner Billingham," I said. "We had a run-in, so to speak. He was a farmer at the time. Things must have changed for him. So, you were going to *'look me up,'* were you? To play cards? Or on general principles? What I want to know, McCool, is what in hell happened to you back in St. Louis? The boys all said you'd been done in, and after you didn't show for a month, I believed it. Word had it your body had been lashed to a log and sent on down the river."

"Damned near right," Claude replied. "They hawgtied me and set me adrift in a canoe. I got sicker than a damn skonk as I was driftin', an' it was two days later when a riverboat hauled me aboard. I'd got myself loose by then, but I was in sorry shape, I'll tell ye. Anyhow, the paddle-wheeler was bound for New Orleans, and this child made the best of 'er. By the time Louisiana come, I'd gathered in quite a stake, and so I figured I'd found a good place to work the market."

"Why in hell didn't you ever come looking for me?"

"I did, lad, I did at that. But when I got thar, ye were already gone—an' better off without me, so far as I could see. I got reports back from time to time, an' after that I never heard no more. I mean, until that rumor of a gambler named Ace Tanner north in Oregon. I'd have come looking eventually, because that's my nature."

I nodded. But one or two things still didn't fit into the puzzle.

"I have my sources too," I said. "As good a grapevine as there is, I'd say. The card thief's communication system. How is it I never once, not in all these years, heard anything about Claude McCool?"

"Changed my name, o' course," Claude said, taking pinch of chewing tobacco. "How about Aristotle Grumbling, ye ever hear o' him?"

"Why shit," I said, "you mean to say that you're Grumbling, the famous wizard of the monte table?"

"At your service, Jesse Tanner. Aristotle hisself."

I thought about it for a moment and then burst out laughing. "Fate and the goddess of luck!" I said. "Here's to her!"

"Luck's okay," Claude grinned (and I made note that he'd lost a few teeth since the old days), "but a Member o' the Order of Black Jack has to help things along at times. Since you're still making a livin' in the same way, Jesse, I figger ye don't jest rely on luck, beautiful though the damsel may be."

"Call me Ace." I nodded. "That's how I'm known. And Johnny Mankiller here—I've had to put a few fellas under."

"Heard about that," McCool said. "Some say that Ace Tanner's a pure killer. What about that, lad?"

"Not true," I replied. "But right now, that's exactly what I'm fixing to do. As I told you, this Jesus Piedra, one of Micheltorena's cutthroats, he stole my woman, and I have every intention of putting him under."

McCool was silent for a few moments, and I couldn't think of anything else to say either.

"The Little Apple, eh? Way I've heard it, Jesse, she's his wife. One of his wives, that is. According to the rumors, he's got three women and half a dozen kids. She say whether she had any kids of her own? But lad, if Piedra's got a dozen men with him, that's less than half of what he's supposed to be able to command. And you're fixin' to ride right to the Fortress? Exactly what are we goin' to do when we catch Piedra, Jesse, or ain't I supposed to ask? For that matter, are you even sure that the lady wants to be with you an' not with Jesus?

He provides for his people pretty well, from what I've heard, an' like I say, she may have a pup or two."

The thought of Manzanita being a mother did in fact disconcert me a bit, since I'd never thought of her in those terms, but it's not my nature to back off once I've set my mind to something. Or maybe all along I'd been thinking of Manzanita Huerfano being Manzanita Tanner and eventually the mother of some heathen children of my own. Sometimes a man's mind plays funny tricks on him when he's not on the lookout for surprises.

"That's simple enough," I replied. "When I catch Piedra, I'm going to kill him. The man owes God a death, and I'm the bounty hunter. Besides that, the only choice I've got is to let the word get around that the bastard *cholo* sonofabitch took one shot at me, wounded the woman I'd won fair and square, and then sneaked up on me and bound me to a damn tree and left me for dead. I ask you, Claudius my friend, would I ever again be able to hold up my head in public? Think on it. But none of this is your doing, and so perhaps you'd best let me be about my business. Now that we're both in California, fate's bound to bring us back together again."

"That a fact?" Uncle Claude said, removing his sombrero, taking the brim between his teeth and running his fingers lightly over the scar on his head.

"Itch, does it?" I asked.

"So you'd have me desert ye? Then how'd I get yore body back so's I could bury it proper? Answer me that."

I laughed so loud that Berutti was actually startled. He turned his head back to see what the devil was going on.

"Let the turkey vultures and the condors dine on my liver," I said. "If a man's got to go, there's no way better as far as I can see."

"She-it, Jesse. Hyar I taught ye everything I know, and fifteen years later ye still don't know diddle from daddle. If we're goin' to commit suicide, I say do 'er right. We beard the lion in his den, *sí, amigo?*"

"*Mais oui.*" I nodded. "That is what we shall do. A bluff's one thing, but a Colt-Patterson's another. If that won't pull it off, perhaps a Sharps at two hundred yards will settle the score. . . ."

Berutti agreed. I could tell.

Late the following afternoon we stopped at Fort Tejon at the foot of the pass road, and as luck would have things, the blacksmith was able to furnish me with some extremely valuable information. A band of ne'er-do-wells had camped alongside the creek, below the fort itself, and the next day a singularly attractive young Indio woman, one who appeared to have been severely beaten by a lover, had led her pony to the gate and had been admitted. Her mare had thrown a shoe, and the smithy had cleaned the damaged hoof and nailed a replacement shoe into place. The Indio woman, whose name the smith did not know, then proceeded to purchase some few things at the post store and had returned to her band of ragtag friends. The bunch of them had ridden southward, the smith said, toward the Tejon Pass.

"Not sure whether we just got some good news or bad," Claude said, whistling through such teeth as he still possessed.

"Mr. McCool," I said, "now that I've found you again, I sure as hell don't want to be responsible for getting you killed."

"Ain't this hound dawg that the Meskin bandido's got a grudge against. Mebbe I'll jest get the drop on ye an' turn ye over to Señor Piedra. Hell, lad, I guess you'd be worth a hundred dollars or so. An' the net result would be just about the same, after all. On the other hand, I've lived long enough already, an' I can still handle a Colt—if I can manage to see what it is I'm shootin' at. We struck out west together. Now we can finish together. I see a certain—how do ye say?—a certain poetic justice in that."

I nodded, but not in agreement. Truth was, I had no intention of letting Jesus Piedra get the drop on me a third time. Johnny Mankiller had begun to snort in his holster, and that was a good sign. It had been a spell since I'd added any new notches.

The trail, easily discernible once again, now veered off to the west, along a lateral ravine that fed to the main drainage. The sky was an intense blue, and three great-winged condors were sailing magnificently overhead. The woods changed character as we worked our way upward, intertwined canyons, rock formations, with the oaks and digger pines of the lower elevations giving way to growth of ponderosa and Oregon hemlock. Bush lupines were still in bloom farther up, and the mountain meadows were lush green—attractive enough that we stopped to allow Berutti and Oppy to tantalize their palates a bit.

"Think those condors might be contemplating us, lad," McCool said. "Not much to pick off my bones—just gristle and sinew. It's you they're watching, Jesse. After your friend Piedra hangs our arses, the big birds'll come take the jelly out of our eyeballs, sure enough."

I glanced at the huge, soaring birds—and shared Uncle Claude's notion that we were being watched by those keen avian eyes.

"I've thought about it more than once, Mr. McCool. There are worse ways to go. A coward dies a thousand times before his real time comes, and the last time must be something of a relief. But to take lead in the chest, your own pistol smoking in your hand, out of tin, out of luck—that's the warrior's vision, the fate of Hector, Achilles, El Cid. . . ."

"Ah, these heroic figures." Claude chuckled, spitting tobacco juice onto a newly blossomed frond of purple lupine. "For you, perhaps, Jesse Tanner. But for myself, I have grown old and silly. No Achilles for me. I'll settle for the admirable Don Quixote, the lantern-jawed knight of La Mancha. But I pray they do not put me in a cage. Well, as my friends the Cheyennes used to say, 'It's a good day to die.' Let's keep moving, lad. How much further do you suppose this trail will lead us? Appears to me we're danged near to the top of some mountain or another. . . ."

We moved ahead, rounded a heap of granite boulders, and there, clinging to the next ridge over, to one of the lateral slopes of what had to be Monte Piños, was a small village—a scattering of shacks arranged about a kind of central courtyard consisting of a corral, a stable, and a garden where corn, melons, and beans were growing.

This is it—the Fortress, Piedra's hideout. . . .

I lifted a hand to point, but before I could in fact utter any words, some other words were spoken:

"Hey, gringos! *A qué hora es la fiesta?* You come eat with us, maybe. Or maybe we have you for dinner, *sí?* Unbuckle your gun belts, señors, *por favor.*"

The welcoming committee was headed by none other than Juan José Raymondo Garcia, as skinny and as ugly as ever.

Uncle Claude glanced at me, nodded.

"Figger the lads mean business, Jesse. Guess we play for time?"

"Exactly my thought," I replied.

Eight

PIEDRA SETS
THE STAKES

There was New York Jake, a butcher boy,
That was always a-getting tight;
Whenever Jake got on a spree,
He was spoiling for a fight.

One day he ran against a knife
In the hands of old Bob Cline—
So over Jake we had a wake,
In the Days of 'Forty-Nine.

There was Hackensack Jim who could outroar
A buffalo bull, you bet!
He would roar all night and roar all day,
And I b'lieve he's roaring yet!

One night he fell in a prospect hole—
'Twas a roaring bad design—
For in that hole he roared out his soul,
In the Days of 'Forty-Nine!

Swarmed over by Piedra's men, we were brought to the outlaw leader. Jesus, blustering with confidence on his own terrain, in his own remote village high on the mountain, surprised the devil out of me by demanding a rematch at cards.

"Señor Tanner, I cannot say that it is good to see you. Ah, well. My men have been keeping the eye on you ever since you left Fort Tejon. When anyone begins to look for Hidalgo Village, we take that to be our business. Unfortunately, you have found us, and if I let you leave, you may be tempted to direct others to our hideout on the mountain. Did thees old man come along and untie you before the sun could burn out your lungs, Gringo Tanner? Now I may have to kill you both."

"I was obliged to look you up," I said. "You took my woman. You didn't pay for what you took. Manzanita Huerfano is mine, Piedra. You gambled, and you lost. The wager was your idea from the beginning. A couple of your men were there, and they know. As I see it, you're honor-bound to return her."

Piedra grinned, then glanced at his men. A few of them had understood what I said. As Claude and I looked from one set of deadly eyes to another, we realized that everyone present would be pleased to disembowel us and use our intestines to tie us up for target practice. These men were not, one might suppose, the gentlest band of *caballeros* who ever lived in Alta California.

"*Sí,*" one of the boys nodded, "I was there. Thees gringo won Manzanita in a card game, and afterward we had to steal her back."

"It was not stealing," Piedra said. "I merely possessed once again the woman who belonged to me."

"Even among thieves," I persisted, "when one loses at cards, the result is final."

Piedra rubbed at his mouth.

"Yer goin' to get us kilt, sure as bearshit," Claude whispered. "Easy, Jesse."

"Is the *anciano* your father, Tanner? Maybe I let you kill him as the price for your freedom? What do you think of that idea?"

"The woman is mine," I said. "But if you wish to play some more cards, amigo . . ."

Piedra broke out laughing. "You have read my mind. Why do you think I have allowed you to come this far? We could have killed you back along the trail—whenever we wished to do so. Instead, I have brought you here so that we might play cards once again. I could not kill you until we have settled the issue between us."

I scowled at Piedra, glanced sideways at Claude. "I'm listening. What choice do I have?"

"You don't got no choice, gringo. You listen to me. I tell you about Manzanita the little dog. She is good to stick, but the world is full of such women. If she had been loyal to me, she would have cut your throat when she had the chance. Instead, she lets your horse loose, and I see that he found his way back to you. Now that we have returned to Hidalgo Village, I will have Little Apple tied over a wine barrel for a day maybe. I let my men fuck her as much as they want, and after that I put a bullet into her brain. She's no good to me no more. Then I leave her body out for the coyotes, since she likes them so much. The old man—he your father, or what?"

"That I am," Claude said, "after a fashion, ye might say. I taught Jesse hyar most of what he knows. We come to California together."

Claude was evidently playing his own game—working the odds, as he himself understood them.

Piedra studied Claude and then stared at me, as though waiting to see if I'd say something to dispute what McCool had asserted. From its sheath he withdrew a Puerto Vallarta fish knife with a ten-inch blade, briefly ran his thumb across the edge, grinned, and began to pick at his teeth.

"Didn't see you at Mokelumne Hill, *anciano*. Why you want to lie for thees Tanner? He's just a goddamn card thief. Maybe you one too, so you stick together? Eh, gringo, you like this knife of mine?"

Piedra's men looked ugly. Half a dozen women in simple garb, a couple with infants in their arms, as well as a small army of children of various genders and ages, now huddled about curiously, eager to see what it was that the leader would do with these two Yankee intruders—and their animals. One young man in particular, I made note, had his eye on Berutti.

Manzanita Huerfano, however, was nowhere to be seen. How in hell did I know she was even still alive? What the smith said at Fort Tejon, of course, but . . .

Piedra used his knife to point first at me and then at Claude.

"All right, gringo. Here's what we going to do. You got no stake. You got nothing to gamble with. But I play one hand with you anyhow. Let's say you got thees worthless dronk at least—use him for a bet. Hokay. I play you the Indio against your *companyero viejo*. If Jesus wins, he require you to kill the two of them if you want to save your own life. If you win, Gringo Tanner, you take the Indio dog and go. I allow you to enjoy her for a little while, then I track you down again and cut off your *cojones*, and the old hombre's too, if he's still around."

"Go for 'er," Claude said. "Don't be concerned none about this *viejo* white beard. At my age, a little while longer ain't goin' to matter. This child's on his way to meet his Maker in any case. Socrates drinks whatever pizzen he's offered an' then passes on."

"Professor McCool," I replied, "there may be one or two slight differences between your charming self and the ancient Socrates."

"O' course they is," Claude replied. "For one thing, I'm a whole hell of a lot better-looking. I've got women as will testify to it."

Piedra was picking his teeth again.

"*Tú y yo,* we play cards? *Sí?*" With these words he turned abruptly and stode off.

I was ushered into the largest of the ramshackle cabins, one constructed partially of adobe bricks, and took a seat at a plank table that was, in fact, the work of a genuine craftsman with a drawknife and an adz. The thick cedar surface had been saturated with some kind of oil, possibly linseed and tongue oil in combination. The floor was composed of adobe bricks set tight, and the surface was hardly worn at all.

Jesus Piedra sat opposite me, while to one side stood Claude McCool and to the other side a teenage boy who may well have been one of Piedra's own. Piedra called for tequila, and a jug was brought. He took a single swig and offered the tequila to me. I nodded and pretended to take a hefty drink myself, tipping back the jug and snorting properly afterward.

"Goddamn new deck of cards, *chinga*! Box ain't never even been opened before. Fifty-fifty, even up, honest."

"Half of one, six dozen of the other," I replied. "Where's the girl? How do I know she's even still alive?"

"Damned *norteamericanos* don't trust nobody." Piedra laughed, his white, square, horselike teeth showing under his curled, mustachioed upper lip. He gave a signal, and Manzanita was brought out from an interior room. She was in the company of two older women, both of whom were distinctly overweight—though possibly neither of these other "wives" was more than thirty years of age.

"Show the gringo your titties," Piedra said.

Manzanita shook her head but said nothing. Piedra gestured to the other women, and one grasped Manzanita about the neck and the other tore the Indian girl's green linen blouse open. Piedra's men laughed, and the outlaw leader used a tallow candle to light the remnant of a cigar, the tobacco now reduced to a stub.

"The old guy got any titties?" Piedra asked me. "What? You don' feel so brave without your *pistola*? I protect you, Ace Tanner. Don' worry, *non inquetante*. Now we play cards, eh? The five-card stud, faceup . . . My boy, he deals the cards. Hokay?"

I motioned toward Uncle Claude. "My partner gets to examine the deck, I take it?"

"Shu, Jes, why not? Brand new cards, made in Cuba, just like this cigar. You wan' smoke, gringo?"

I declined.

"Then let's play. . . . The old man, *el anciano*, against my Injun *vaquilla*."

The boy shuffled the deck several times but showed no especial dexterity in the process. If Piedra wanted to control the fall of the cards, I thought, he'd possibly picked the wrong dealer. Or else the young fellow was simply trying to allay any suspicions on my part. But what would have been the purpose of that?

I thought about those condors circling against the intense blue of heaven, and I thought about the cries of coyotes I'd heard the previous night. Mostly I stared fixedly at the boy who was dealing the cards. I could see fear in his eyes. What would his life be worth in the event that Jesus Piedra lost? Was this not such a man as would murder his own son?

Piedra's men gathered about now, and the sheer physical presence of them was nearly sufficient to choke the breath out of me. Even through the blur of words I caught a reference to hanging a man by his feet and having him beaten to death by the women. I had to use every bit of concentration I had to prevent my hands from trembling. Cold sweat was on my face, but I managed to drum my fingers on the table and wink at Piedra.

All the world's a stage, and all the men and women merely players. . . .

My first card was a jack of hearts, while Piedra's was a king of diamonds.

Then, like fate itself, aces, one after another, came down on my side of the table, while Piedra's hand was a complete zero, nothing in suit, not even so much as a rotten pair of anything.

A deathly silence hung in the room. Smoke and the ᵧ̵ of whiskey were suspended, and I found myself thinking of currant jelly in glass bottles. Jesus stood, snuffed out the cigar against the bare brown skin of the young man's shoulder. He, in turn, winced, gritted his teeth and did not cry out. The boy had, apparently, learned his lessons well.

"*Chinga tu madre!* Fuck-king gringo! God has spared your life, and yet He torments mine," Jesus sputtered—and then crossed himself.

From the voices in the room, I could tell the nature of the sentiment among Piedra's men. But the outlaw cahuna, to his own credit, overruled them and stuck to his word.

"I let you go this time," he said, spitting on the floor. "This time you win fair. Juan José, get these men their horses and weapons. You, Tanner, you take the Little Apple for a while. Use whatever holes she has, I don' care. Make some more if you don' like what she's got. After a while I will find you and win her back. It will give me time to think of really good way to execute her, and you too. Follow them, Juan José, until they are out of our goddamn mountains. . . ."

Piedra's other two wives pushed Manzanita toward me, and she stood there, eyes downcast. Her face, I noted, was badly swollen, one eye nearly closed. Apparently, Piedra had been amusing himself with her.

"Juan José will follow you and kill you once we are close to the Tejon Pass trail," Manzanita said. "I think he is on the ridge above us even now. Jesus told you one thing, but he will do something different. That is his way."

Deuce, I noted, was still limping slightly, despite the new shoe. I suspected a minor separation in the hoof itself. By all rights, the mare should have been put out to grass for a couple of weeks at least. Limp or not, however, I could tell that Berutti was pleased as punch to be back with his new friend. For a moment I toyed with the mental image of the two horses standing together in formal dress, with possibly Claude's white mule, Oppy, reading from the Good Book: *I now pronounce you Horse and Mare, and may the nongod of the Houyhnhnms look over you and allow you to prosper even as you bear these human creatures about from place to place.*

The idea occurred to me because I'd actually read the entire book of *Gulliver's Travels* just a couple of years earlier, and not merely the part about Gulliver being on the island with the little people.

"Thanks for sending Berutti back to me," I replied. "Without my horse, I'd never have caught up with you."

"Perhaps it would have been better if you had not found me again, Ace Tanner. I am nothing but bad luck to you. Bad luck is what no *gambolier* needs."

"You're not going to admit that I saved your life? Why, I believe Jesus meant to do away with you—that's what he said, in any case."

"He would never do such a thing," Manzanita replied. "Not as long as there are other men who would want me. Jesus is a very good businessman."

"Expect the little lady's right," Uncle Claude remarked. "There's somebody up above, no question on 'er. If I wasn't a hunnert years old, I'd climb up through the tan oaks an' bushwhack him."

"Figured as much from the beginning," I said. "Just the one, you guess?"

Claude nodded, glanced sideways at the slope. "Piedra give us back our guns, but not our ammunition. For all the hardware, lad, we might as well be a couple of kids. Just movin' targets."

"Under my saddlebag," I said. "Caps, powder, and lead slugs for my thirty-two. An Injun told me I should always carry a few spares, just in case."

"Injun, hell, Jesse Tanner. I'm the ringtail coon as told ye that. Good of ye to remember an old man's advice, though."

"We'll stop in the draw," I said. "Under cover of

those poplars. While the ponies are sucking water, I'll get my pistol loaded and ready for action."

Within a mile or two of the wagon road south across the Tehachapis, a rifle ball thunked into the dirt in front of me, causing Berutti to rear back—not enough to throw me, but certainly enough to get my attention. A moment later we heard the echoing report of what turned out to be a long-barreled Kentucky rifle, the weapon being handled by none other than Juan José Raymondo Garcia.

"Head for them live oaks!" Claude sang out, just as though fifteen years had never passed us by and he was still the adult and I was the kid setting out with him for a great adventure, the adventure called life. But he was right, of course. That was precisely the logical thing to do.

Piedra jest wanted ye out o' his territory so's no alcalde an' a bunch o' vigilant outraged citizens or a company of bluecoats would be snoopin' around by Monte Piños, that's all. Piedra never meant for ye to escape, an' mebbe he intended to get rid o' the Injun gal at the same time.

It wasn't Claude talking, I could see that. The elder thief was altogether too busy hightailing his white mule toward the comparative safety of the trees.

Another shot rang out, but I never did see where it struck. Little Deuce, with Manzanita aboard, was right alongside of me. And then we reached cover—had dismounted and tied the horses more or less out of harm's way.

"A gnat must of gone up that coon's nose just as he fired," Claude said. "He's on the rim above, sure as hell. An easy shot, when you think of it. He should have had at least one of us dead to rights, an' that'd be you, Jesse Tanner. I don't figger he's got any real grudge against me."

"Maybe just a warning, then," I suggested.

"Warning, hell, Jess. More likely, he's jest toying with us."

Manzanita was standing between two of the horses—Deuce and Berutti—possibly with a thought to using the animals as a barricade. Berutti looked doubtful.

"Can we get out of here, Ace Tanner?" Manzanita called to me. "You think it's just Juan José, or are there other men now?"

I glanced at the Indian girl and once again felt that strange, excruciatingly pleasant sensation that seemed at once to be centered both in my loins and in my brain. Somehow I had the damnedest time trying to think straight when she was near me. And this was a woman, for God's sake, that I'd never even touched in a familiar way. At that moment, indeed, nothing made much sense.

"He'll keep us pinned hyar," Claude said, "either until some of the other boys show or until we decide to make a break. Lad, I don't like the odds much."

"Me either, Claude. So what we need to do is cut into those odds just a bit."

"Use the gal for bait?"

"You goddamned reprobate, McCool. You haven't changed a bit."

"Ain't no one ever told me why I should."

"You men stop babbling and think of some way to save us. That's what men are supposed to do."

"Nice-lookin' shiner," Claude said to Manzanita. "Was ye badgerin' Señor Jesus, or did he jest pop ye on general principles?"

"I'm going up there," I said.

"If anyone goes, it'll be this coy-ote. Lad, you stay hyar."

"There's some jerky in the saddlebag. Chew on that, McCool. If I'm not back by sunset, use the twilight to make a break for it. The fort can't be more than a couple of miles. Take my stallion—let your mule run along behind."

I had sufficient lead and powder, but only four caps, but with these I partially loaded my Colt-Patterson. I winked at Manzanita and then bolted off into the brush—was astonished to feel my face go red. I was actually blushing, for God's sake.

Keeping low, and sometimes crawling beneath tangles of greasewood or toyon, I worked my way steadily up the slope.

On hands and knees, and midway through a dense tangle of brush, I found myself brought short. My heart was pounding and I could barely catch my breath. A large porcupine was no more than a yard in front of me, and since I was crawling, at almost eye height. We stared intently at one another, each puzzled by the other's identity, each attempting to determine whether the other posed any kind of threat. When I was a boy, I believed (because I'd been told by adults) that porcupines actually were able to throw their quills by means of lashing their tails back and forth. A porcupine quill in the eye would doubtless blind a person and possibly bring on death, since the quills were barbed and hence inevitably worked their way back into the living tissue into which they'd been thrust.

Since the porky seemed not of a mind to do so, and since under the circumstances I could hardly shoot the creature, I myself backed away. The porky pawed the ground, seemingly quite proud of himself for having driven off this grotesque four-legged creature it had surprised in the bush.

Had I not been looking as I crawled ahead, I might well have reached out and put one hand squarely on the porky's back—and my venture to the rim, to take care of Juan José Raymondo Garcia, would have been foiled.

Eventually the spiny creature shuttled off through the tangle, and I remained on hands and knees, resting a moment to allow the beat of my heart to slow. My face was suddenly covered with sweat. The fretful porcupine, I concluded, would have made a hell of a poker player—except that his bluff was, in fact, not a bluff at all. Not even the mountain lion, so those who know contend, will do battle with a porky. The marmotlike fisher, a high country weasel, is the porcupine's only real enemy, other than humanity. A hell of a suit of armor.

I backed up a few yards and then began to move ahead once more in a direction opposite to what my sudden acquaintance had taken. I'd just begun my new progress when I heard a rifle discharge—one shot, one shot only. Apparently Garcia was intent upon keeping his targets pinned down but was not in any particular hurry. Indeed, his actions seemed almost those of a playful boy who happened to have a high-powered rifle at his disposal.

After another twenty minutes of wriggling my way upslope, I found myself on the rocky crest of the ridge, perhaps two or three hundred yards from where I estimated the tall man to be.

I moved cautiously along the rim, from rock tumble to rock tumble. I could see plainly the live oaks below me. Astonishing, I mused, how little actual distance I'd covered, though in the process I'd reached a height perhaps five hundred feet above the trail along which we'd been making our escape.

High above, riding the heavens, was a single huge condor, as well as a pair of either hawks or eagles or vultures. Whatever they were, they seemed mere midgets compared to the king of birds—although I recall being told that a golden eagle in fact is more than a match for a condor, should the two big birds have a disagreement. The eagle's formidable beak and talons more than compensated for the size differential. As for the condor, magnificent though he was, this bird lacked the hunting talons of the eagle—talons sufficient to disembowel at a single raking thrust.

In any case, there appeared to be no conflict in the sky above. All three birds glided though wide circles, as though performing exercises in celestial geometry, so to speak.

Once more I checked the cylinder of my pistol to assure myself that the hammer would not fall on one of the two empty chambers.

Pistol in hand, I moved forward, crouching, taking no chances of being prematurely discovered.

Then he was there before me, but with his back turned and his horse nowhere in sight. I surmised the animal was tied short somewhere ahead, perhaps back over the rim so as to remain hidden. Garcia's Kentucky long rifle was resting across a slab of granite, and Juan José was kneeling behind, hunched forward, apparently in the act of drawing careful aim. Possibly he had in mind to kill the horses so that his prey would have to flee on foot. From such a point of advantage, a skilled marksman might well be able pick off human beings, even at this distance. But horses and mules made much more satisfactory targets.

I worked my way around some boulders so as to come up precisely behind my man. With Juan José just a few yards distant and his back entirely turned to me, I stood to full height and took dead aim.

"Good afternoon, señor," I said, making a valiant attempt to control the intense anger I felt. "Please do not move, or I'll be obliged to fire. *Comprende, amgio?*"

Garcia put down his rifle, half raised his hands, and slowly, deliberately, turned around.

"You do not shoot me in the back? Señor Tanner, it is you? I mean you no harm. Jesus, he told me to make sure that you do not return to Hidalgo Village, that is all. . . ."

At six-foot-six or so, but rangy and weighing perhaps no more than a hundred and eighty pounds, Juan José was nonetheless a striking figure of a man, broad-shouldered, his vaquero's shirt hanging about his shoulders like a draped flag or a tent. He would prove to be a challenging prisoner, I could see that. At some point I would likely find it convenient either to turn him loose or to shoot him.

He grinned, glanced into the dull blue of heaven, taking note perhaps of the three big birds overhead, and then lunged forward, drawing his horse pistol as he did so. Garcia's reckless act nearly caught me by surprise. In point of fact, he got off his shot, something I should never have allowed him to do. Our pistols exploded at nearly the identical moment, but his shot, made even as he was lunging, went wide, while my own aim was quite accurate. The slug from Johnny Mankiller struck Juan José full in the throat. He fell forward in the gritty sand and dry weeds, his head thrashing back and forth. The pistol flew from his hand, arced through the air, bounced from a broken chunk of granite, and was still. His dark blood jetted out and pooled into the rough-grained sand, leaching back into the earth. The mouth was open, gasping for breath.

The tall vaquero lay dead.

I glanced heavenward, making note that the condor was no longer visible. Then, out of the corner of my eye, I caught a sensation of movement. I spun about, pistol in hand, ready to fire once more.

But the new arrival was not human. Instead, there was the condor, perched in ungainly fashion astride the upper branches of a slim scrub oak, the immense wings fanning softly as the bird attempted to achieve its balance.

"Good afternoon, Death Bird," I said, chuckling with relief. "Allow me to retrieve Señor Garcia's pistol and rifle and two or three other things, and I'll depart and leave you to your grim business."

The condor, as if in response to what I'd said, stretched out its wings and held them in avian cruciform, at the same time hissing at me repeatedly.

"Not to worry, big fellow. I won't take anything that's valuable to you. You don't have need of the pony, do you?"

Get out of here, Yank, and let me eat.

I holstered Johnny Mankiller, took the dead man's weapons and ammunition belt, and then began to search for the horse, which I was certain to be close about.

The condor spread his sails and glided earthward, gracefully alighting next to the corpse. As I watched, the big bird paced back and forth, as if estimating the extent and nature of this prize.

What, I wondered, had become of the two vultures that so recently has shared sky with the condor? Had they gone to alert their friends?

I located the horse and started back from the mountain, leaving the great-winged black bird to its secret repast of human flesh.

N i n e

UNCLE CLAUDE
DISAPPEARS
AGAIN

'Twould make our Eastern people rave
To see both great and small,
The old, with one foot in the grave,
All "splurging" at a ball.

Wait for the music,
Wait for the music,
Wait for the music,
And we'll all have a dance.

On foot they through the diggings wind,
And over mountains tall,
With young ones tagging on behind,
Flat-footed, for the ball.

Wait for the music,
Wait for the music,
Wait for the music,
And we'll all have a dance.

A dozen babies on the bed,
And all begin to squall;
Their mothers wish their brats were dead,
For crying at the ball.

Wait for the music,
Wait for the music,

Wait for the music,
And we'll all have a dance.

We rode north, heading for Coarse Gold, and I realized that, one way or the other, time had come for me to determine what direction my life was to take from this moment onward. Was a leopard capable of changing its elemental spots, particularly when the beast was back in company, so to speak, with the grand papa Leopard? Was I, in fact, beginning to get *religion*? Was the influence of my father, the Pennsylvania preacher, from whose house and whose authority I'd long since run away, beginning to have its effect on me? My own illegitimacy and the fact that the Man of God who sired me chose never to honor my ma with the blessings of marriage nor me with the favor of legal claim to my own last name—none of that made a difference. Notorious gambler and expert on horses and women, Jesse Ace Tanner was beset with images of himself as the owner of a small farm, perhaps over in the Napa Valley or beside the waters of the Rio de las Plumas, near Oroville. He could see himself sitting in a rocking chair, and across the room from him, knitting before an open fireplace, was—who? There was no one doing the knitting. Instead, it was Manzanita Huerfano, and she was playing her guitar.

Coon, ye forgot to get the lady her git-fiddle.

She rode in front of me, and I urged Berutti ahead, drew alongside.

"I neglected to ask Piedra for your music box with strings," I said, intending these words as an apology.

"Jesus, he busted the *guitara* a week ago," Manzanita replied. "I will buy another when I have the money to do so. Right now, Ace Tanner, I am angry with you. Why did you have to win me at cards once again? Why did you follow us? Everything would have been all right, *muy bonito*. I took the big chance when I turned your horse loose, and for that Jesus punished me. But then he was getting over his *cólera*. Soon he would have wished for me to lie down with him again, in the way of a man and his wife. Then you show up, and now everything is ruined, *averiado*. You want me to be free, as you call it, even if I don't want to be that. You want me to be on my own, though that is not what I desire. And now that you have killed Jesus' close friend, Juan José Raymondo Garcia, he will track you again—only this time he will probably kill you and me also."

Manzanita's outburst astonished me.

"Quiet, you two," Uncle Claude grumbled from behind us. "Ye'll wake the b'ars an' the catty-mounts."

Berutti reached over, nipped at Deuce's mane. For her part, the mare ignored him totally.

"Do I follow you now, Gringo Tanner?" Manzanita demanded. "Do I become the woman, the mistress, of the Yan-gee card *ladrónes*? And when Jesus or someone else shoots you in the back, how then shall I bury you? Yes, that will happen one day, and we both know it."

"How would you have buried Jesus Piedra? I'd say that fellow's days are definitely numbered. Those that can't abide a hackamore are fated to end up with riatas around their necks. Piedra and Murieta hanging there, side by side—that's my prediction, unless Johnny Mankiller gets him first. Little Apple, are you saying that you wish to return to Hidalgo Village? In that place you'll become old and fat and worn-out, with half a dozen children, worthless in the world's eyes, by the time you're thirty-five, which is how old I am right now. You can see what's happened to the women who string along with the Joaquin Murietas of the world."

"Jesus and Joaquin are not the same person, Ace

Tanner. Besides, we women know how to survive. For now I am thought beautiful by the hombres. When that is no longer so, then I will act as though I were a mother to the young vaqueros. That is how it has always been for women. As for the men, they have always grown old and fat and worthless. You pretend to see the future, but what you see does not give me fear. Besides, that thirty-five, it is a long way off. Perhaps now that you have won me again, you wish to get rid of me. Is that so? All right, then, but I will not return to Hidalgo Village. Just now I have decided that. Instead I will buy myself a guitar and sing for a living. I don't need any man, not if he doesn't want me. You men are all the same. You are disgusting goats. Perhaps God should get rid of all of you."

"Get along, you kids," Claude McCool sang out. "Behave, damnit. Pretend you're civilized. Keep yore eyes peeled. A fella never knows. . . . Little Apple, this child can tell ye for sure, it ain't long from twenty to thirty-five. Fifteen years, it goes past in a wink, an' that's true about life in general. Ain't nothin' permanent about 'er."

"If a rattlesnake bites you once," Manzanita said, smiling, suddenly friendly as all the world, "it's the snake's fault."

I waited a moment, and then my curiosity got the better of me. "Yes," I replied. "And if the snake bites you a second time?"

"Then it's your own damn fault, that's what."

I nodded. "Do you have to act shitty?" I asked. "Or is that simply your nature?"

"*No hablo inglés.* I am coyote. I am Miwok Yosemite. Your insults do not touch me."

"Techy as a young carcajou with bad feet, ain't she?" Claude put in. "Little Apple, my lady, don't ye pay no attention to Jesse. He had bad teachers. He says good things about ye in private, though, in case that makes any difference. Says ye learnt Latin an' such. Mebbe somethin' about poetry as well. For an iggerant dawg like Claude McCool to hear of them things, it's damned impressive, that's what. Though I guess gals is always better at schoolin' than boys. When Jesse was a kid, when the two of us first hitched together, an' even before that, when he was jest a whippersnapper, he was always readin' one book or another. Dime novels, for instance, an' things like *The Iliad* an' *Don Quixote* as well. Mebbe the two of ye have got somethin' in common after all. Other than being young an' in love, I mean. . . ."

Claude had been building to that final line, and if I'd seen it coming, I might have cut it short. As had been the case so often in my life, I'd given in to listening to the words come melting out of his mouth. Claude McCool had the gift of gab, no two ways about it.

"He's not interested in thees *Indian girl*," Manzanita said, her tones subdued now. "He just feels sorry for me, that's all. Wants to rescue me from Piedra. Wants to rescue me from God Himself. Has bad judgment. Now that he don't need to rescue me anymore, he will lose interest. I don't trust him."

I glanced at Claude, shrugged.

"Women," I grumbled. "Manzanita says that so as not to hurt my feelings. Hell, I didn't expect her to fall in love with me. No man in his right mind wants a damned trained spaniel following him around. There are plenty of ladies about, as far as that goes, even in California. Tell her I said she's free to go whenever she wants to. I've got no claim on her—and no use for someone who doesn't care a fig about me. I'm a professional gambler, for crying out loud. No way I'm going to get myself tied down."

"Yankee men don't know how to treat women!" Manzanita said. "Tío Claudius, you tell him to talk to me if he wants to talk about me. Otherwise I don't pay no attention."

"Double negative," I laughed. "Tell her she just doubled her negative. She may know Latin, but she doesn't know beans about *inglés*. Mr. McCool, I'm riding ahead—see if I can find game. I've had enough of jerked beef and half-cooked elk. Some good fresh meat . . ."

"Men are all the same," I heard Manzanita saying as I nudged Berutti forward and then off the trail toward a stand of big valley oaks half a mile off.

"Don't even think about using those spurs," Berutti said. "You want to run, we'll run. Just take it easy on this stallion's sides, if you please. Claudius, he's in love with her too, you realize. If he weren't a hundred or so, he'd be on his knees begging her to marry him. I'm just saying what's obvious to anyone with horse sense."

"Guess I saw that one coming, but I thought the cat had your tongue," I replied.

"If I've been kind of quiet, it's because I've been thinking. Why don't you buy a thousand acres—or maybe just win some land in a card game—and we'll raise cattle? I always wanted to be a cow pony. Out on the trail after roundup, that's the life. . . ."

"McCool's in love with a mere child?"

"You ain't blind, are you?"

Then Berutti fluttered his lips, whistling as he did so, and I knew the conversation was over.

Perhaps Claude was smitten with the Indian girl, but whatever the case, he chose to nag at me—and the refrain ran thus: make an honest woman of her, marry her, settle down, forget about card playing, marry her, study for the law or else get elected sheriff in some town of promise, like Stockton, for instance, get married. . . .

Manzanita continued in her more or less unpleasant frame of mind as we rode northward through the San Joaquin Valley, resting during the heat of the day beneath whatever big water oaks were nearby, and continuing on into the twilight. The girl was sharp-tongued and generally rebellious, and a couple of times I reiterated that she was free to go her own way.

"You're going back to the goldfields," she said, "and that's where I want to go too. So I'll stay with you for a little while. That way you can rescue me some more."

As we were resting the afternoon of the second day, Manzanita turned toward me and smiled beautifully.

"Gringo Tanner," she said. "Maybe I like you after all. Even if you don't know *nothing* about Latin."

"One of my many failings," I said, first drinking from a canteen and then offering her some water.

She declined.

"If ye know Latin, then for Gawd's sake let's hear ye say somethin' in 'er," Claude said, sucking air through his teeth. "That Latin's real pretty, as I recollect."

Manzanita smiled again.

Damned if she isn't a damboosa one, my occasional voice said, *pretty as any wild orchid.*

"*Omnia Gallia est diviso in partes tres,*" she nodded. "*Amor, amas, amat.* Ace Tanner works *pro bono. Morituri te salutamus. Quo vadis,* gringo?"

"I think I smell false Latin," I replied.

"She sayin' three's a crowd?" McCool asked, turning to me.

"Translate, if you please," I said.

This time Manzanita's smile resembled that of the Mona Lisa.

"I merely admitted that I owe you three debts," she nodded. "I will repay you when we get where we're going—I will sing songs for the miners and earn money. The Yankee miners, they are very generous—if the lady treats them right."

"You sure that's what you said?" I asked, scratching at my sideburns.

"Of course. Why would I wish to tell you something that is not so?"

"Think this gent'll head for Monterey," Claude said.

"What are you talking about, Ancient One?" I asked.

"You kids may not be interested in matters o' the heart, but Claudius Pennyworth McCool is. Or doesn't a fella my age get to have a social life? Ye see, it turns out that I've got some important business with a certain widow woman who owns a big house, a *casa grande*, not far from the mission. She's lonely, it seems like, an' wants me to stay with her."

"Goddamn it, Uncle Claude, we've just gotten back together after all that time when I thought you were dead. I've got to see if my cousin's actually in Coarse Gold. After that we can ride on over to Monterey if you wish."

"I'd jest be in the way, lad. You two are better off without me. I'm jest bad luck, always have been. An' like I said, the widow woman's been in my thoughts a powerful lot lately. . . ."

McCool woke me early the following morning—at least an hour before sunrise. The stars were just beginning to fade in the east, and westward the waning quarter moon hung translucent and silver above the barely visible rims of the Coast Range. Coyotes were yapping a mile or so away, downstream along the San Joaquin River.

"Hate to disturb your beauty rest, lad, but I figgered it'd be bad manners to jest disappear—considering how long we was apart the last time I did that. You awake, Jesse?"

Claude, I realized, was holding his hands up, grinning at the same time.

Only at that moment did I realize I was clasping Johnny Mankiller. I nodded, returned the pistol to its holster, and crawled out from beneath my sleeping blanket.

"What in hell are you talking about, Claude?"

"The widow woman I was telling ye of. I dreamed about 'er last night, so I knew it was time to make tracks back thar. You an' the Apple, you're better off without a geezer like me crampin' yore style. As she says in that foreign language of hers, three's a crowd. Where in hell do those Latins live, anyhow?"

Uncle Claude liked to play dumb. For all I knew, he understood whatever it was Manzanita had said—if she'd actually said anything at all.

"You miserable bastard," I protested. "You go helling off to Monterey, and I won't even know when to come bury you."

"I'll outlive ye, lad. I swear it. Now listen here— don't go waking the leetle gal. I'm heading to Monterey, an' that's all there is to it. I'll meet ye in Coarse Gold in a month. Ye got my word on it. Make a point o' being thar. Might be I'll have a surprise for ye. An' watch out for that Butterfield feller—jest keep yore eye peeled is all. The fella had a mean look about him, like someone set on gettin' even."

"Billingham?" I responded.

"The very man, lad."

I tried to protest further, but it was no use. Claude McCool had something on his mind. I could see it in his eyes.

"Coarse Gold in a month," I said as he mounted his mule.

Once in the saddle, he bowed from the waist and gave me a flourish of his sombrero. "Bed 'er, lad, or there'll be another man who will. *Bonjour* an' all that."

"McCool, you old sonofabitch!" I yelled after him. "You be there!"

Manzanita was up by that time—was standing beside me.

I turned to her, gestured. "He's off to see the widow lady," I said. "*Claudio tiene fama de ser un veleta.* He's always been that way."

"Now you pretend to speak Spanish, Ace Tanner?"

"Just *pretend*."

"Will Claude McCool come back after a time?"

I nodded. "Bad pennies always turn up."

"So he has a friend who lives beside the big Kuku, the ocean? I also lived there for a time—for two months, there at the mission. Then I was taken back to San José. Perhaps Claude is a Kikuna, one of the water people."

Far to the east, above the half-visible ranks of the Sierra Nevada, the bulging white rim of the morning sun was now beginning to display itself.

"More Latin?" I asked.

Quite to my surprise, Manzanita placed both hands upon my arm—almost as a child might do to a parent.

"No," she said. "Those words are from the people among whom I was born—the Yosemite Miwoks, the Pohonichi. I remember very little, I'm afraid. If I ever returned to those people to live, I would have much to learn. The priests who raised me always said that we Indio children should forget our languages—learn the new one, *español*, or even the Latin. That way, in the years ahead, we could become citizens of Alta California, for we were part of Mexico then. After that we had our revolution, and then the Yankees came, the Bostons. And then came the gold."

She was quiet for a long moment—as though she felt she had revealed too much. Finally, when the silence had lasted longer than felt comfortable, I said, "*Manzanita* is Spanish. Do you remember your—Yosemite name?"

"Hekeke, the quail," she said. "I was to be a *miwü* called Hekeke-osa-be, the quail woman. But sometimes I was called Mayenu, and I suppose that is why the friars began to use the name Manzanita."

I nodded, watched as the sun pulled free of the eastern horizon, a great bubble of endless white fire that came out of the earth. A flock of crows that had spend the night in another grove of water oaks, just downstream from our camp, now began to leap off into the air, first one or two at a time, then groups of half a dozen all at once. In not much more than a minute, they were all gone—to wherever it is that crows go just after sunrise. In Pennsylvania, I recalled, they found green pastures and spent their days hopping about among the cows, with occasional time out for gossip sessions in the elms.

"What does Mayenu mean, then?" I asked.

"I do not know, Ace Tanner. But *miwü* means person, and Miwok are the people. I told you how the cowboys killed my parents and then gave me to the mission, to the priests who saved my life. But I was only a little girl when that happened. There is much that I do not remember, and perhaps there is also much that I have chosen not to remember. But always I believed that one day I might return to the Pohonichi. I have remembered some of the words, but not all. I remembered because I wanted to be able to speak when the time came. The chief of those people, the *Tokahayapo*, is called Tenieya, as I told you before. I remember Tenieya, though he was not the chief when I was a small child. At that time he was the leader of the hunters. But perhaps this Tenieya is someone different, I do not know. That was fifteen years ago, and much has happened. Now there are white men everywhere, Californios and Yankees alike. The Miwoks used the word Walums sometimes, and sometimes Saldu, though my people knew a little bit of Spanish as well. Sometimes our young men would work for one of the ranchos—they would move the cattle around or search for animals that had strayed back into the mountains. Don't worry about your friend, Ace. I think he will return. You are part of his family."

"Hope so," I said, turning back toward our smoldering campfire. "Let's heat the coffee, have a bite to eat, and head on out. The mountains are calling."

I guess it was Claude's leaving that finally broke the ice between Manzanita and me. In any case, we found ourselves drawing closer, because I guess the truth was we were attracted to each other. I damn sure was attracted to her, I know that much. Manzanita liked playing with words, of course, and that didn't change. But now she insisted that I not only owned her by virtue of having won her twice at cards, but also because I had saved her life. Hence, she belonged to me three times over, and that meant she would have to be my personal servant for thirty years.

She chattered away as we rode, and I guess I talked too. In fact I told her I was thinking about settling down, of becoming a proper burgher, like my cousin Jamie Savage—if the fellow I'd heard of *was* my cousin.

Before we knew it—that is, before we'd realized the significance of it—we'd half constructed a proper rancho, built on homestead land. Only when we found ourselves beginning to quarrel lightheartedly about how the formal gardens were to be laid out did we realize what we were doing—and we both began laughing senselessly, like a couple of giddy children.

By afternoon the valley heat was terrific, not hot and muggy, the way things sometimes got in Pennsylvania or Missouri, but hot and so damned dry that neither man nor horse was up to sweating—the kind of hot it gets around Taos or out on the Mojave. We rested through a portion of the heat but then decided to move onward, with the promise of sundown to lure us ahead.

Those big towers of cumulus that formed daily above the Sierra, a hundred miles more or less off to the east of us, had begun to drift out over the valley, and the possibility of a summer downpour became significant. The dry grass, as dead as it appeared, seemed miraculously aware that something was about to happen. Manzanita and I could both smell it in the air—an intoxicating odor, like wine fresh out of a burned barrel.

Then, just before sundown, there were clouds overhead, and lightning began to flash off to the east—and then closer and closer. Berutti was nervous, and he turned his big square head back in my direction as if to ask me what the hell was going on.

"Head for the trees," I shouted to Manzanita. "The heavens are about to split open. Your Catholic God lacks temperance!"

"The lightning will hit you, Ace Tanner. But perhaps it is just Coyote?"

"One of the saints, is he?"

"Yes, that is true. If you speak your blasphemies, I will not ride near you. It is too dangerous!"

But she was laughing.

"My father—Reverend Tanner—he never taught me about St. Coyote. Let's get to cover!"

Manzanita leaned forward, whistled in Deuce's ears, and urged her mare toward the oaks.

Sure as the devil, raindrops began to spatter on the ground: millions of raindrops the size of pollywogs.

The dry grass of summer, in response, gave off showers of aromatic perfumes. I half expected to hear music welling out of the earth itself.

Ten

Uzmati Comes Calling

I suppose you have heard all the talkin'
Of the very noted horse thief Joaquin;
He was caught in Calaveras,
But he couldn't stand the joke,
So the Rangers cut his head off
And have got it in the soak.

Now I warn everybody not to ramble,
Never drink, never fight, never gamble
Or you'll never have a cent,
All your money will be spent,
And you to Sacramento
To the prison brig be sent.

They took three-fingered Jack
And cut his hand off,
Then the Rangers drove the rest
Of the band off;
Next they took the head and hand,
And they had 'em well-preserved,
And the Rangers got the credit,
Which they very much deserved.

Joaquin, just before he was taken,
Killed a Chinaman and stole his bacon;
Then he went down to Sonora,
Where he killed eleven more-a,

And a damned big Digger Indian,
Which made the twenty-four-a.

You have heard of the steel
He wore 'round him,
I will tell you what it was
When they found him,
'Twas a long-tom iron,
To protect him in his crimes;
And they swore by the holes,
He'd been shot a thousand times.

Now I warn everybody not to ramble,
Never drink, never fight, never gamble,
Or you'll never have a cent,
All your money will be spent,
And you to Sacramento
To the prison brig be sent.

We'd been a couple of hundred yards from the oak grove when the rain began in earnest. By the time we reached the relative protection of the trees, our clothing was drenched, and we were wet to the skin. I have seen such an intensity of rainfall only two or three times in my life, before or since. Laughing and joking, we tethered our horses back under the overhang of the heavily leafed boughs, and then, as if by spontaneous inclination, we fell, still laughing with the uncontrolled frenzy of children, into one another's arms. We were both taken by surprise, I think. Surely I was. Astonished at how good and right it felt for me to be holding this woman—and at the same time how amazingly small, even delicate, she seemed to me at that moment. I breathed in deeply the damp odor of her, of Manzanita herself, as if to fix that aroma for-

ever in my consciousness. Damn it anyway—I'm trying
my best to tell you how I felt at just that moment, and
I know I'm doing a poor job of yarning. Maybe it
felt—well, the way it was supposed to feel. But now,
for an instant at least, what I'd imagined hundreds of
times and yet had tried hard as hell to avoid imagining
had happened—and what more might transpire as a result of what had already happened I was scared as hell
even to think about. And, yes, I know that none of this
makes the least sense, except maybe to those who have
experienced the same kind of thing.

I mean, Manzanita wasn't just any woman—not to
me, she wasn't.

She was trembling noticeably, and I don't think it
was completely because she was soaked to the skin and
we were in the midst of one hell of a thunder and lightning storm.

She threw her head back, and water was dripping
down her face and catching at the corners of her
mouth. Her silver and turquoise coyote medallion
gleamed with a sheen of moisture, and for a crazy moment I even imagined the damned thing's tongue was
hanging out. Likely it was just my own imagination. In
any case, I couldn't resist the temptation, and as if by
instinct I leaned forward and placed my lips on Manzanita's. She didn't resist me, but she didn't respond either. Fearful that I might have violated this new bond
of closeness between us, I drew back then, as if to assure her the kiss had been playful—or an embrace of
friendship. She was staring straight at me, and I found
that I could not meet her gaze.

I laughed nervously, and she pursed her lips, half
closed her eyes.

"Let's get a fire going—get dried out," I suggested,
not certain what else to say.

Manzanita Huerfano nodded.

"All girls have dreams," she said mysteriously—and
then turned from me as I let go of her.

• • •

Confusion raged through my mind. Truth is, I'd never known quite how to treat a woman I really cared for. With señoritas in cantinas or with those who were *putas*, I'd never had any trouble—possibly because the ladies themselves knew exactly what they were about, and all a gent had to do was to follow their leads. Everything's a hell of a lot easier if the other person knows just what to do next. In any case, it was an ancient dance, a ritual enacted endlessly from the beginning of human time—a man and a woman, both aroused, both wanting something, even if the something happened to be different enough to make you want to cry. My whole life, so to speak, had been one of pretense and bluff. Success, you see, lies in knowing the deck and in keeping an absolutely straight face, in lighting a cigarillo at just the right moment, in seeming always in complete control.

I thought about a certain young wife in Oregon City, a few months earlier, a wife who'd braved entry into the tavern where her husband Abner, a big, broad-shouldered fellow who probably wasn't any brighter than he needed to be, was sitting at a card table across from me, one among several. This gal—Flo Billingham, I think her name was—actually grabbed her husband by the hair and pulled him over backward onto the floor. I tell you, I'd rather have faced a rabid cata-mount than the fury of that woman. As she stood there over her half-drunk husband, she pointed at me without hesitation: "Your kind," she said, "you've got no feelings. No one's at home behind that smug confidence. You've taken my man Abner's money, but it's my money too. It's wrong, even if you was as handsome as Satan hisself, except that you ain't!"

A cowboy or a miner with a gun in hand, that kind of thing I can handle. But the wrath of a wife whose husband has gambled away her egg money, that's too much for this card thief.

The fellows in the tavern gathered around us, of course, and now everyone started laughing and whooping and pounding each other on the back. The young wife, faced with dumbass male unity of response that might have been translated as "By Gawd, we're all in this hyar together," turned and stalked out of the room. Abner, he got to his feet, started an apology, and then took off after his woman.

The following afternoon, as I was riding out of town, there she was—and I half expected her to have a pistol in hand. Instead the lady let me know in no uncertain manner that she intended to have a bit of dalliance with the gambling man. Afterward, as we lay together at the edge of a newly mowed hayfield, she bit at the hair on my chest and laughed.

"Only right that I should get something out of my man handin' over his stash, ain't that so? I can't see why the ladies shouldn't be allowed to have a little on the side if they want it. What's good for the goose. . . ."

I nodded, stood up, pulled my breeches back on, and buttoned my shirt. I reached for my jacket and for Johnny Mankiller, where I had hung the two of them over the branch of a little madrone that was growing close by.

When pretty Flo had once again donned her skirt and blouse and turned to me as though for a parting kiss, I pressed a fifty dollar gold piece into her hand. She stared at the coin and then winked at me.

"If I could get Abner to pay such wages," she said, "I'd be a rich woman. You figger I was worth it, Jesse Tanner? Oh, I know your name, all right."

I mounted Berutti, tipped my hat, and rode off.

"You're a phony sonofabitch," my horse said, nonchalantly shaking his head and snorting.

This episode flashed through my mind as I fumbled with a couple of twists of still more or less dry grass and some dead leaves from under the big oak, got my flint striker to work, and blew between my hands at the struggling flame.

Even thinking about that Oregon City woman made me feel guilty—and, what else? Disloyal? But such a thought was insane.

Manzanita turned, gathered more fuel—anything that wasn't already wet, and within a few minutes we managed to achieve a commendable fire that provided a significant degree of heat.

We stood side by side, warming ourselves, watching as St. Coyote or Gawd Himself put on an absolutely amazing display of lighting across the sky. Rain, heavy rain, continued to fall. But westward, out over the coastal mountains, there were still no clouds, and so the orange-red light of sundown streamed in through the downpour. Altogether it was like something out of a dream, only the actual experience was better than any dream ever could have been.

At that moment lightning struck very near us, perhaps no more than a hundred yards distant, drawn, perhaps, by the presence of one lonely digger pine that had rooted itself close by the riverbank.

And a frenzy of blackbirds just then, hundreds of them drawn into a flock, but out of season, unheard of this time of the year, came streaming across the grass-land, darting first one way and then the other as if the individual birds had somehow been formed into a sep-arate and complete organism of their own, a shining, hunting dragon that glided above the earth's surface in search of something—but what? Approaching the spot where Manzanita and I stood, side by side, the black-bird creature shattered apart into all its constituent particles, as though in an explosion of gunpowder that had gone off around us, with the two of us in its midst, and yet there was no noise, not the least hint of a sound, and then the birds coalesced beyond us, once again forming into the hunting creature, and disap-peared beyond the line of oaks and cottonwoods off to the north of where we stood, the two of us entranced and more than a little bewildered. Only maybe I'm getting carried away in describing what I remember. Let's just say it was *beautiful*.

"God forms a strange pack of hunting dogs," Manzanita said—and then burst into a peal of high, shrill laughter that I could feel more than hear because of the continuing downpour.

She turned to me then, and this time her eyes were not pleading and were not simply confused. They demanded that I—well, that I do something after all, because as she saw it, that was the correct portion for the male. A man was supposed to *do something*, even if that something turned out to be wrong.

Thus, I took her in my arms and kissed her full on the mouth. For a long moment I feared that I had mistaken the signs she'd given me—that she'd be insulted, and I, the professional gambler, had just confirmed her generally low opinion of male animals. Yet perhaps it was, after all, more a matter of surprise—and of Manzanita herself being not quite certain what to do, part of her mind at war with the other portion. Or perhaps mind itself, at such a moment, simply ceases to work very well at all.

But then her fingernails were digging into my back, quite noticeable even though my jacket and shirt, and I realized that her mouth was open as it pressed against mine, as though granting me entry, giving permission for further liberties. Under the circumstances, what was a gentleman to do?

We kissed for a long while, the two of us exploring this newly discovered territory of our feelings for one another, hungry for the touch, the smell, the simple electric presence of man and woman together. I swear, there's no magic greater.

When we finally drew apart, holding one another at arm's length, we became aware the digger pine that had been struck by lighting was in fact burning—its uppermost limbs on fire, and not even the continuing rainfall shot through with final light of the day could quench those flames.

"First we eat, and after that . . ." Manzanita said, her voice trailing away. "And after that, *una celebración.*"

The rain continued for several hours, though the thunder and lightning were by now diminished—rather had trailed away to the north, for an indirect brightness, reflected from the clouds, still came to us occasionally. But the thunder was far away and sounded much like the metal rims of a dray, heaped with hay or sacks of feed, crossing back and forth over cobblestones.

Employing what remained of my fabled boyhood tree-climbing skills, I managed to string a pair of saddle blankets from one oak limb to another—something I deemed necessary, inasmuch as even the thick foliage of the big oak didn't provide an altogether adequate shelter from the rain. Everything was wet by now, and the water was making its way to our little oasis around the campfire.

Berutti and Deuce managed somehow to pull free of their pickets and, once loose, came to get closer to their human keepers, and in fact seemed determined to join us around the campfire. I rose to tend to the horses, but Manzanita indicated that the equines should be allowed to remain.

"They're not afraid of the dark, you know," I protested, but I could tell that my words would have no effect whatsoever.

"*Norteamericano jugadores,* they do not know about such matters," Little Apple replied, smiling. "This a beautiful evening, rain and all. The world around us smells new, Ace Tanner. It is wonderful, *asombroso.* Why did you not demand that Jesus should give you my *guitara*? How can I sing if I do not have my *instrumento*?"

I was nearly certain that Berutti and Deuce had exchanged a significant glance. Hadn't she said quite specifically that Piedra had smashed the guitar? Had she actually forgotten, or was she just trying to get my goat? Or was she saying something quite different? For myself, I lit one of my last two or three cigarillos, savored the flavor of the smoke, and stared out into the summer darkness. It seemed to me that life itself might be compared to seven-card stud—except that the Creator never got around to dealing that final card, faceup and shining and exactly the card a fellow's looking for. Or if He did, actually did dole out just the right card, then the hand was over, and stakes were already on the table for the next go-around. A case might be made that God was the house dealer, one whose mind simply is not on the game. The game itself is irrelevant to Him. He wins one way or the other. In the meanwhile, the whole business of human life might be likened to a series of small bursts of brilliance, anticipated, looked forward to with either joy or fear, but then, finally, anticlimactic as hell.

Yet the beautiful *señorita* sitting across from me in the firelight? Would this event also prove to be simply one more highly anticipated but not very significant episode? For both of us? Or would one or the other come away keenly disappointed?

If only a kay-hoona had some real idea about how his life was going to turn out. However, if he did, then I guess there couldn't be any anticipation. How did that philosopher term things? *Life's a bitchkitty, a real, honest-to-Gawd bitchkitty.*

What in hell was I supposed to do next?

I stared at Manzanita, studied her features, noted how the firelight caused her coyote medallion to glow—only I knew that wasn't really possible. Just an illusion. Perhaps this whole thing was just an illusion.

"Give me your flask of *aguardiente*, Jesse Tanner. All this rain makes me wish to have a drink of the whiskey."

"Good idea," I said, rising, stumbling to where I'd stashed the saddlebags.

"You take too long!" she called out.

"Patience, woman, patience!" I called back, astonished actually at the tone of my voice—as though we'd suddenly become an old married couple, utterly used to one another and willing to jibe back and forth.

I brought the flask of whiskey and we stepped back under the now wildly flapping blanket—wind was blowing, a warm, wet, utterly intoxicating wind. We drank, laughing like idiots as we passed the flask back and forth, and then, as I turned to place the container on the ground and heap half-dry fuel on the fire, Manzanita leaped onto my back.

"You are my stallion, Gringo Tanner. . . ."

Then we were on the ground together, kissing, searching, and she wrapped her legs about my middle.

"I'm going to make love to you," I said.

"Yes," she answered. "Hurry, *mi alma,* hurry, hurry . . ."

After some scrambling about to get half naked, a scrambling that neither of us would really remember afterward, she took me in her hands and guided me into her. And we were together, our bodies working their ancient rhythm, moving together and then away, together and then away.

When it was over we lay side by side for a long while. The fire had dwindled to little more than embers, and I rose, stumbling, pulled my breeches on, and managed to find a few clutches of dry leaves and twigs to place over the coals.

Then we lay together once more and between us we emptied the flask. Manzanita fell asleep in my arms, me half drunk with the elixir of life and half drunk with the nearness and the odor of this woman who had, without even trying, so utterly grabbed hold of me.

She slept, and with her in my arms, I listened to the continued falling of the rain, made note that the horses had apparently opted to sleep standing up—in deference to the storm, presumably—and then I fell into the warm wet darkness as well.

But the night wasn't finished with us.

A damned grizzly, Uzmati ("You-zem-a-tee," Yosemite) in the language Manzanita had spoken as a small child, came to raid our camp, on the prowl for good salty bacon, something of which bears seem inordinately fond. The two horses took fright—reasonably enough. Deuce broke her tether and clattered off into the darkness. As for the griz, he (or she) was searching for bacon, like I said, or for other viands, mostly out of mischief, and all I could think to do was to yell at the top of my lungs and fire off two or three shots from Johnny Mankiller, not with the intent to wound or kill the bruin, for very real danger might well have lain in that course of action, but rather to scare the beast off. That's the problem with grizzlies, the characteristic that would eventually bring them to the edge of extinction: it's just not in their nature to be much afraid of any living creature, including human beings. Indians are said to heap stones over those who have been killed by the grizzlies, the body left where it was found. And those who passed by, for many years afterward, would add a rock to the heap. In this fashion, I guess, they reverenced the spirit of the bear and the spirit of the human as well.

Anyhow, with a flaming branch of dead live oak in one hand and my pistol in the other, and Berutti making an awful ruckus all the while, I managed to drive his bearship away. Or possibly the griz had simply tired of the game and decided to be about its business, I don't know.

By dawn we set out to apprehend the wily Deuce, but the little mare didn't seem of a mind to allow herself to be captured easily. But the rainstorm was over, and the clouds, or what remained of them after the fine frenzy of the previous night, had drifted away eastward. Sunlight streamed over everything, and damned if the world didn't seem altogether new.

Finally, after numerous dodges and dashes, the mare leaped out into the deep, slow-moving waters of San Joaquin River, and Manzanita and I, like two shouting children, leaped in after her. We turned her about and managed to drag her in to the riverbank, where I used my lariat to cinch her to a toyon bush.

"We will have to take off our clothes and dry them over the fire." Manzanita laughed.

Then we were there on the grassy bankside, kissing and nipping and clawing one another and by God just plain in a mating frenzy again. Damned if I know what got into me, but I found myself kissing her belly, and then . . .

Well, hell, you've made love before. No point in my telling you how it's done. Anyhow, if you haven't, it's best if you learn for yourselves.

The short of the matter was that Manzanita got into such a dithering trance that I was half afraid she was going to have a heart attack and die of apoplexy right then while I was using my tongue on her.

Afterward, we fell asleep again, locked in embrace, and when we woke, we both felt like we had hangovers. The sun was a third of the way up the sky, and the August heat was beginning to settle in once more.

For my part, I'd taken to dreaming about a piece of land and a house and a by-Gawd barn, maybe a green one just to be different. It would take me six months of concerted and careful gambling, as I calculated matters, in order to get together a sufficient stake. In my mind's eye—or in my imagination, I should say—this crazy little Indio gal, Little Apple, Mayenu-osa-be, Manzanita Huerfano, she'd surely agree to be my wife, inasmuch as things just wouldn't be right any other way.

I'd already gambled enough in my life, to be sure, and about this one thing I did not wish to gamble.

We rode toward the mountains, and Manzanita told me a bit more about her people, the Yosemites, a southern branch of the Miwoks as I gathered things. She spoke of the possibility—just an idle fancy, to be sure—of returning to live with those people. But at the same time she realized the impossibility of it. For Manzanita was no longer Indian in her mind and hadn't been for a number of years. She was a Californio first, and now, with Yankee acquisition of the land of Alta California, she was an American—or would be soon, since California had been admitted into the Union.

That was something to think of. This wild and beautiful land, California—rowdy, lawless for the most part, uncivilized, a nation of half-crazed gold miners—this land was part of the United States of America and had its own constitution and its own government—even though the place was more like a human explosion than an honest-to-God state.

In point of fact, there was still a great portion of California that remained terra incognita—specifically the immense range of mountains that stretched along the westward side of the Central Valley. Wagon trains managed to cross the Sierra, of course, and men on snowshoes carried mail across in the midst of winter, but the southern end of the range remained all but impassable. Time would unravel the secrets of the place the Indians called Inyo, but for the time being not even the miners had managed to work their way into the highest portions of the mountains.

Or possibly it was just that there didn't seem to be any gold in the high granite of which the Sierra was composed. I'd ridden along the eastern escarpment of the mountains a couple of years earlier. The size and sheer mass of the range was enough to humble a man. And if that didn't do it, why, passing along the upper Sacramento River, from Yreka southward, with Mount Shasta huge and mysterious above, why, that would do it for sure.

Eleven

In Coarse Gold

I well remember those old times,
The days of 'Forty-Nine, sir,
When miners gaily singing went
Into each golden mine, sir.
When buckskin coats and patched-up pants
Were fashions of the day, sir;
And when a mining claim would yield
The biggest kind of pay, sir.

Whack fol de da, ri tol tol lol da,
Te my whack fol de da!

Those highly interesting times
When miners used to think, sir,
That whiskey straight was very cheap
At fifty cents a drink, sir;
And oftentimes would freely pay
Ten dollars for a shirt, sir.

Whack fol de da, ri tol tol lol da,
Te my whack fol de da!

I do respect those good old times,
for men were honest then, sir,
The diggings paid, men couldn't stop
To cheat their fellow men, sir.
This salting and this jumping claims,
Was not considered fair, sir.

You ask a man where you might work,
He'd tell you, "Anywhere, sir."

Whack fol de da, ri tol tol lol da,
Te my whack fol de da!

As we started through the scrub oak and digger pines of the hills to the north of Fresno, close by a hill called Red Top, the two of us as happy and as stupid as a couple of moony-eyed kids in Pennsylvania, our brave new world has given a serious jolt. The whole thing was my fault, to be sure, for I'd let my guard down—I simply was not paying sufficient attention. Manzanita and I were talking about all manner of irrelevant things, mostly just enjoying the sounds of our own voices intermingled, when three masked highwaymen, on foot, in imitation of the notorious Joaquin Murieta, stepped out from behind a chaparral thicket and accosted us there at a point where the wagon trail passed close beneath some big tombstone rocks. In an instant I took note of where the thieves' ponies were tied, back under a pair of low-growing live oaks perhaps fifty yards distant.

"Stand and be damned!" the apparent leader called out. "Drop your weapons!"

All three men were wearing sombreros, and the leader had on a bright red jacket that was, as they say, somewhat the worse for the wear—though by California standards serviceable enough. The men, I realized, were not Mexican at all, though dressed in the Californio fashion. The leader had a mustache that had recently been waxed, while the man's two companyeros were sporting half-grown beards.

I nudged Berutti forward so as to put myself between Manzanita and the would-be heist men, all three with their pistols trained on us. I raised my hands and smiled as pleasantly as I could under the circumstances, nodded to no one in particular, and tipped my Oregon felt hat.

"Gents," I said. "Must be some mistake here. My name's Ace Tanner. If you're up for a game of cards, why I'm your man. Beyond that, I'm afraid I can't help you boys, since my entire earthly fortune's in the bank in Mokelumne Hill. If it's money you're after, you'll have to look for it there. As is, I'm out of lead, out of tin. Even my whiskey flask's as dry as a bone."

"Tanner the card thief? Hell yes, an' I'm the famous Kit Carson. Y'all take me for some kind o' fool?"

"That very individual," I assured them. "The lady here's my wife. We've got four little ones, aged three, five, and seven. They're with their nanny, in Hangtown. That's where we're headed—by way of Mokelumne Hill, of course, so's we can withdraw our money. You're welcome to ride along with us, if you wish."

"Three, five, and seven—hell, that's just three. What kind o' fool do you take me for, mister? Y'all don't look like no gambler to me."

"The five-year-olds are twins," I said. "Little girls, pretty as pictures. Like I was telling you fellows, Manzanita and I, we've got family responsibilities. I'll happily provide your price when we get to Mokelumne Hill. Money's no good to a dead man, after all. How much do you need, gents?"

"Ain't she the bitch from over to San José?" another of the thieves asked his chief-in-command. "The one with the good voice an' the git-fiddle? Jesus Piedra's woman?"

At this moment Manzanita spun Deuce about, let out a piercing whoop, and applied her spurs to the mare's sides. Low in the saddle and with the agility of a trick rider, she bolted away in the direction of the rock formations above us.

Several shots ensued, two of them issuing from the barrel of Johnny Mankiller—as I drove Berutti directly at the highway agents, firing as I did so. Amazingly enough, I found myself unscathed, while the robber in the red coat lay dead on the trail, and one of his henchmen, though wounded, began to run. Half a dozen steps farther along he also expired, even before I could direct a finishing shot to his backside. To tell the truth, I've always been loath to shoot anyone in the back, even under such circumstances as those I've just described. I never do it unless it's necessary—or unless I'm in a jolly mood. In any case, the one who'd taken lead sprawled forward, his leg lashing out three or four times, and then he lay still.

The third of the former trio was running like hell toward the live oak where the boys had left their horses, back when they were still figuring on an easy robbery and a leisurely ride to wherever they'd planned to get drunk and hire a señorita or two.

Sorry it didn't turn out that way. Damned sorry.

I reined Berutti about to determine what had happened to Manzanita—and what I saw sickened me, at least for the moment.

Dead was all I could think.

Deuce was by the tombstone formation, saddle empty. Manzanita had been thrown from her saddle, and her body was draped, so to speak, among the branches of some greasewood brush.

She pulled loose, however, fell to the ground, and rose to one knee, at the same time wiping at a bloody tear on the side of her face.

"I'm all right, Jesse Tanner. That one, he's getting away."

Manzanita pointed toward the rapidly retreating bandido.

I turned Berutti yet one more time and urged him forward in pursuit of our friend.

"Trying to make me dizzy, boss? It ever occur to you that you're likely to get this horse shot when you pull a stunt like this? Dare I suggest you arrange your gunfights so as not to endanger your faithful equine companion?"

"What's that?" I demanded, leaning forward so the stallion could hear me.

I could detect him grinding his teeth as he ran. By then we'd caught our quarry, who'd realized we were coming and now rolled to one side of the galloping Berutti and came up firing.

The man's aim was off, however, perhaps due to the fact that he was out of breath. But mine wasn't as I fired from horseback. This pathetic figure of a highway agent jerked, flopped to one side, and lay still. There was no dignity about him.

The day's only half done, coon, an' ye've already put three gents under. Three o' them, gone beaver, just like that. An' but for the luck o' the draw, it could be you an' the leetle lady what's coolin' out on the sod and making ready to fertilize the grass, like a couple piles o' buffler dung along the Republican River somewhar.

"True enough," I mumbled to myself, putting Johnny Mankiller back into his holster.

I reined Berutti to a halt, dismounted, and walked over to retrieve the man's weapon, a perfectly serviceable Navy-issue Colt.

All in all, three additional pistols would come in handy—or they could be sold at a mercantile. The three horses, three saddles, and the pack mule were also valuable, as were the pony, saddle, rifle, and pistol I'd taken from Piedra's man Garcia, but I'd have to be wary that no one in Coarse Gold (or wherever) recognized the animals—though for all that, highway robbers weren't likely to have very many friends about, not among the miners and merchants upon whom they preyed, at least. In California at that time, I might say, pistols were not as plentiful as is often supposed. Let's just say that the demand sometimes exceeded the supply, and the same was true of many commodities— lumber, clothing, anything that had to be brought in around the Horn or by supply wagon from Oregon country or across from Independence or St. Louis. California may not have been at the end of the world in those days, but it wasn't far from it.

Manzanita's wound looked much worse than it was—a bad cut, probably caused by a sharp twig when she was thrown from her horse. She closed her eyes as I tended the laceration, wincing when I dabbed at it with some horse liniment I'd bought in Fresno on my way south to find Piedra's hideout.

"I know one of those bandidos," Manzanita said, "used to know him at least. The hombre, the *ladrón* in the scarlet jacket. He worked for Piedra for a time, but then Jesus ran him out of Hidalgo Village. We called him Boston Eddie because he was from the United States. I think Jesus had met him in Mexico. Perhaps the two of them were in jail at the same time."

"Had the feeling he might have known you," I said. "Why'd Piedra part company with this Boston Eddie, or do you know?"

"Jesus, he got angry because Boston was keeping too much of the money he stole. Besides that, he bungled a theft of cattle on a big rancho below the Tehachapi Mountains—the rancho that belongs to the one they call Abel Stearns, a *norteamericano* who came into the country years before I was born, when Alta California still belonged to Mexico. Stearns was one of the Californio rebel leaders when we won our independence from Mexico."

We put a few miles behind us before stopping for the night since, for all we knew, the three men I'd killed might well have cohorts not too far away. We veered westward, away from the wagon trail, and came down into the sharp ravine of the upper reaches of the Little Fresno River, a stream which was hardly more than a good-sized creek even out in the San Joaquin Valley. I expected to find a mining camp or two, but as it turned out, the canyon was without human inhabitants. Apparently there were no auriferous gravels along this part of the drainage.

Just about sundown we reached the stream, low in its bed this late in the season. We watched as fifty or so turkey vultures came in for their nightly carouse—roosting in what I supposed to be a favorite black oak, just at the upper end of the meadow where Manzanita and I and our newly enlarged string of horses could camp for the night. In any case, the tree's bark was profusely striped with the white residue of their droppings. The gathering of the clan, so to speak.

If my map was anything like accurate (though California maps seldom were—the main towns and streams being indicated, but with a lot of imagination in between), then we were no more than a couple of hours' ride from the town of Coarse Gold. With luck, we'd be there by noon the following day.

Just above the spot where we rolled out our blankets, the stream came snaking over a bench of serpentine rock that appeared to be veined with glow worms by the yellow-red twilight that was rapidly being swallowed by shadows. At the foot of the waterfall was a considerable pool, a basin hewn in the soft stone by the power of winter floods. A great blue heron rose easily from the shallows as we approached, squawking in minor annoyance at being disturbed while at the business of frogging, and sailed upslope amidst canyon liveoaks, digger pines, and California nutmegs.

"*Muy bonito*, is it not, Jesse Tanner? Now that we have grown to know one another so well, now that we have made love together, why should we not bathe together? Am I shameless, do you think? If you do not wish to do this thing, then I will swim by myself after we have eaten our supper. I will not try to make you do anything you do not wish to do. . . ."

"I take it," I said, "that I don't even get a chance to answer my lady's questions. I'm quite a good swimmer, I'll have you know. The pool looks like it was made just for the two of us."

"When it is dark," Manzanita said, "then you will not be able to see me. I will be clothed in darkness, just as the moon is at the end of its cycle, before it begins to wax once more."

I burst out laughing. "Why, then," I said, "I'll build a campfire right beside the water, a big one. I'll smoke a cigarillo while you're swimming. You'll be Aphrodite rising from the water."

As I was speaking, Manzanita picked up a dry oak puffball and threw it at me, narrowly missing my head.

"No," she said, frowning at me, "I shall be Artemis, the goddess of the hunt. I'll cause you to be Aktaeon, and I will turn all your hunting dogs into coyotes, and they will leap upon you and devour you."

"So it's coyote medicine you've got? And your silver amulet, that's got magic in it?"

"After we have eaten," Manzanita said, "we will come back to the pool here by the waterfall and I will show you my magic."

We made wild love that night—and whether the intensity was caused by the excitement of the bandidos earlier that day or by virtue of the simple fact that we had found ourselves a kind of Garden of Eden, I don't know. Whatever the case, we were nothing if not excessive. We could not seem to get our fill of one another—in the sort of enchanted way that new lovers have.

But when morning came, we found ourselves awkward around each other, awkward and sparing with our words. We took breakfast and then, our animals trailing behind us, rode on toward Coarse Gold.

Whenever a fellow thinks he's got things just about figured out and is of a mind to put his life on a straight course, trouble's no more than a few feet away. If I've got any sort of wisdom, gained through dear experience and the turning of a great many cards, why, I suppose this is it: Whatever cards you're dealt, don't talk about them. Keep your own counsel. And if you've got a dream, don't even admit it to yourself. The fact is, you can't trust yourself any more than another varmint. Human beings have an astonishing tendency to shoot themselves in the foot, as the saying goes. And for Jesse Tanner, that goes in spades—and clubs and hearts and diamonds as well.

Like I was saying . . .

As we rode into the town of Coarse Gold, trailing our little remuda behind us, I began to expatiate on the virtues of good, clean work—and of finding a way of making a living that involved considerably less risk of getting shot than card-thieving entails. I was talking about this sort of thing because, of course, I hadn't yet figured out that it was acceptable for a man, any man, just to ask the woman he's fallen in love with if she'd be willing to share the rest of her life with him, whatever the risks, whatever the chances against the two of them knowing any real material success. At that moment I somehow forgot about the words *in sickness and in health, for better or for worse.* Or maybe it wasn't that at all, but just that I was afraid she'd laugh at me and ride off in search of a guitar.

In any case, she frowned and for a moment looked like a cat that's had its paw stepped on.

"When did I ever ask you to marry me, Ace Tanner? You *own* me—isn't that enough for you? If you're trying to figure out a way of saying 'Adios, Little Apple,' the words are easily spoken. Why do gringos have to beat around the bush so much?"

Since I couldn't think of a single coherent thing to say, I chose not to respond at all. Possibly there's also a certain streak of perversity in the human soul—or maybe that's not really different than our compulsion to shoot ourselves in the feet.

The main street of the little mining town was dusty, though one side appeared to have had a water wagon drawn over it within the past couple of days. Several new buildings were under construction, and from the fresh-cut looks of the timbers being employed, I presumed that a sawmill of some variety had been constructed in the area. A majority of the buildings were put together out of pine or fir logs, skinned, notched at the ends, and grouted with adobe. I made note of a few glass windows, and that meant shipments from back East or from South America were finding their way to Cal-i-forny.

Each of the several saloons seemed to be doing a brisk business, even though the hour was only a little past noon. And a knot of men stood around a buckboard, in the back of which stood an ungainly looking machine equipped with bellows, a couple of gears, and a sprocket chain. My first thought was, *something for the smithy*, though later I'd be told that the contraption was a dry washer, designed for working small amounts of sand and gravel in places where no water was available—since deposits of gold-bearing sands were sometimes found high on the rims above any creek or river.

The odors of linseed oil, creosote, turpentine, sealing tar, and whiskey were all on the air as I surveyed the signs on the various establishments.

SAVAGE MERCANTILE. There it was. Very soon I'd know whether rumor had been correct—whether my cousin Jamie Savage was indeed the proprietor.

For a moment I could almost see myself waiting on customers in my cousin's store. Hell, Jim Beckwourth himself had spoken of owning a similar establishment in the town of Sonora. If that mountain man, fur trapper, and occasional horse thief could tend store, then why not Ace Tanner? Indeed, word had it that none other than Pompey Charbonneau was tending a hotel of sorts near Placer Dry Diggins.

In all likelihood, it was time to settle down. In fact, Manzanita had just dismounted and tied off Berutti and Deuce to the hitching rail, and I was thinking about precisely that—settling down, I mean—when I heard a vaguely familiar voice call out, *"Ace Tanner, that's you, ain't it? By Gawd, I'm fixin' to shoot you like any dog in the street. Turn around and meet your maker, you gawddamn sonofabitch wife-humpin' card cheat!"*

Abner Billingham, was it him? Drunk out of his damned skull and six hundred miles from his home in the Willamette Valley?

"Some guys are bad losers," Berutti said. "Heck, boss, you know that. Ain't that why you pack the pistol?"

I gestured for Manzanita to get back behind the horses, and then I turned, slowly, deliberately, to face whatever the hell sort of complication had chosen just this moment to invade my life.

With a practiced motion I nudged the cloth of my jacket back away from Johnny Mankiller. The sun was slightly behind me and thus would be, to a certain extent, in the eyes of whoever it was that was calling me to battle.

No question about it. Johnny was chuckling, chuckling. He lived, as I knew well enough, for moments precisely like this one.

Don't misfire, you sonofabitch. Today is definitely not a good day to die.

Twelve

WORTHLESS YELLOW METAL

I heard of gold at Sutter's Mill,
At Michigan Bluff and Iowa Hill,
But I never thought it was rich until
I started off to prospect:
And brighter burned gold fever, lads.

When I was a young'n and in my prime
I used to prospect all the time—
The more I dug, the more I panned,
The more I studied the river's sand,
The brighter burned gold fever, lads.

At Yankee Jim's I bought a purse,
Inquired for Iowa Hill, of course,
And traveled on—but what was worse,
Fetched up in Shirt-tail Canyon:
O, brighter burned gold fever, lads.

When I was older and had more gumption,
I got real patient and had no conniption—
I found my way to Greenhorn Creek
And dug out nuggets as big as your cheek:
The brighter burned gold fever, lads.

'Twas true, of course, the mining ground
Was staked and claimed for miles around,
And nary a bed was to be found

Though I had nuggets by the pound—
Yes, brighter burned gold fever lads.

Black sand and mica and pure iron sulfides
They didn't fool me for bony-fides—
Then came a nugget the size of an ely-funt
And I was so rich I had the smell of it:
Still brighter burned gold fever, lads.

I walked slowly toward Billingham, since that's who it was, all right. For his part, he continued to jaw-bone at me, as though intent upon attracting the greatest possible degree of attention from our fellow pilgrims there on the main street of Coarse Gold. When we were perhaps twenty feet from one another, I stopped and set myself.

"Friend," I said, "if it's a rematch at cards you want, why, I'm your man. I'd rather take your gold than give you my lead, and that's a fact. If there's a score to settle, let's do it the honorable way—with a deck of cards. I've taken out more than thirty men, and I've no desire to make you number thirty-something."

In truth, I hadn't made it quite to thirty as yet, but I figured *more than thirty* would sound both authentic and intimidating. My reputation, after all, was quite well-known—and had been the talk of the town back in Oregon City. Folks up there tend to be more civilized, less given to excessive behavior, if you see what I mean.

"Go for your gun, you bastard!" Abner Billingham shouted.

I shook my head. "Your deal," I said. "Make your play or get off the street. I've got business to attend to. . . ."

Billingham gritted his teeth and threw back his head.

A sudden gust of wind lifted his felt hat into the air and sent it spinning along the dusty thoroughfare.

A miner, with no shirt on but with wide blue suspenders sporting silver buckles holding up his randomly patched britches, broke into a loud guffaw, though why the fellow should have found the spectacle of Abner's hat sailing along the street in the least bit humorous I'm sure I don't know. Some guys would laugh at Grandma's funeral.

I kept my eyes directly on my opponent's right hand—a hand that hung there, full of apparent indecision. Clearly the man was drunk, for otherwise he'd never have acted the part of such a damned fool. As anyone this side of Taos might have testified, if you want to shoot down Ace Tanner, you ought to do it from behind, and with a good bit of cover to boot.

"Well?" I demanded.

"Aw sheet!" Billingham muttered, and then went for the gun.

Johnny Mankiller jumped into my hand and in an instant I had drawn on the former Oregon clodbuster. He seemed engaged in a kind of ritual dance, dancing with himself, playing the roles of both partners all at once. The poor devil couldn't free his weapon from its canvas holster, as though the pistol's brass sighting nib had become entangled in the heavy threads with which the sheath was sewn.

Just look at that incompetent jackass, Johnny Mankiller mumbled. *Hardly worth wasting the lead on him. . . .*

"If you manage to pull that peashooter loose from its moorings," I said, "you're a dead man. Give up on it, Billingham, and I'll buy you a drink—give you a chance to recoup your losses, whatever they were."

You ain't forgettin' about his wife, are ye?

But the man glared at me, gritted his teeth, and yanked the six-shooter from its holster.

The boys along either side of Main Street began to cheer.

I fired. I really had no heart to kill the hombre, but when someone's waving a firearm, a fellow doesn't actually have any choice in the matter. Billingham dropped to both knees, cursed one last time, fired into the air, and slumped forward, facedown.

Manzanita ran forward to where Billingham was sprawled in the street. I holstered Johnny Mankiller and walked slowly forward.

"Dead." The Little Apple nodded.

Within what seemed to be no more than a few seconds, the law had arrived. It was none other than Mike Bonner, whom I'd met a few months earlier, on the Trinity River. Bonner was a roustabout that few men cared to cross—and at the time I'd met him, he was a prospector, a man more interested in hunting for gold than in actually finding it. I didn't bother to ask how it was that he happened to be wearing a star on his chambray shirt. In California, those days, things tended to happen at random. Hell, Joe Meek himself had practiced medicine for a year—simply because he'd learned the art of extracting lead from the human body.

"What ye doin' over this way, Ace? Been playin' cards with this fellow, have ye?"

"In Oregon City it was," I replied. "Manzanita Huerfano and I, we were just riding into town, and this man, Abner Billingham I believe his name is, insisted on fighting."

"Ain't allowed in Coarse Gold," Bonner said. "That's why they done hired this child."

The shirtless miner came forward on my behalf.

"Jest like the dude says, Constable. The dearly departed, he started the whole thing. I was hyar from the beginning. The gambler thar, he had 'im dead to rights but didn't shoot. The corpse, he wouldn't give in—finally got his fusee out an' that's when he quit breathin'."

"Anyone else see what happened?" Bonner yelled with a voice sort of like gravel in the midst of thunder.

He had an air of authority, did Mike Bonner. Then several fellas came forward and backed my story.

Bonner nodded. "Ace, ye got some cash to pay for a burying? I'd be much obliged. . . ."

"It'll be arranged," I said. "Good to see you again, Michael."

"Yep. Well, keep that damned gun o' yours whar it belongs, you hear? Otherwise, you'll be paying for yore own grave-digging."

I can see that this story's getting out of hand. In fact, it's doing its damnedest to turn into some sort of saga—or get as long as one of those Russian novels you hear about. So let me speed things up a bit.

Turned out that the Savage Mercantile was indeed owned and operated by none other than my own cousin Jamie—though I hadn't seen him since we had been boys together back in Pennsylvania. Sometimes our families would visit, and when that happened Jamie and I got on like thieves, so to speak. I always figured Jamie had things better than I did, since his ma and his pa were legally married, and all that. Also, Jamie's pa had a dairy farm and as far as I could tell was a lot nicer to be around than my own pa. Once I even asked if I could go live with Jamie and his folks. Ma cried, and Pa found good reason to whip me with a horsewhip. Usually I yelled like the devil when I got beat on, but that time I gritted my teeth and didn't make any sound at all.

Uncle Claude, he just laughed when I told him about it, and before long he was yarning about the time he and Bully O'Bragh escaped from the Pawnees. The Pawnees, or so Claude claimed, still practiced cannibalism in those days and were planning to roast him and O'Bragh and have a dinner in their honor. . . .

But back to the story at hand.

Jamie Savage, as it turned out, was among the leading men in the town—and perhaps even in the state of California itself, for he held the rank of major in the volunteer militia called the Mariposa Battalion. He and Mike Bonner were not only on friendly terms, but even occasional drinking and hunting partners.

Once Jamie and I had officially claimed one another as kin, with much back-pounding and irrelevant conversation that did its best to pick up where we left off when we were in our early teens, my cousin turned to Manzanita.

"What in God's own name have you done to this girl, Jesse? She looks as though she'd been rolled down a mountainside."

I explained briefly, omitting the detail of killing three would-be robbers, and Manzanita nodded demurely.

I left Manzanita in Jamie's company and made my way to the town stables, where I was able to sell the newly acquired horses for a fair price and where I placed the four extra pistols and one long rifle on consignment.

When I returned to the Savage Mercantile, I was surprised—and not altogether disappointed—to learn that Manzanita had asked for a job as clerk in the store and that Jamie, who had been one person short for the past couple of weeks, had given her the position.

"Makes sense, when you think of it," he told me. "The men who're looking for work stay on just long enough to get a stake, and then they're off to investigate the latest rumor of a strike. Manzanita says the two of you are planning to stay in Coarse Gold for a spell?"

I made note of a certain guitar suspended from a pair of pegs on the wall behind the main counter. I nodded to Manzanita, glanced at the instrument, and said, "Think I'll buy that git-fiddle for a friend of mine. How much is it?"

"Am I the friend you're talking about, Gringo Tanner?" Little Apple asked.

"The very one," I replied.

Jamie grinned and scowled all at once, then winked at me.

"Can't have my clerks insulting the customers, young lady. We don't call Americans gringos, we don't call Injuns diggers, we don't call Nigras colored, an' we don't call Meskins greasers. Here in the mines everybody's equal as long as they've got dust. Remember that the customer's always right unless I say otherwise, or at least until we get his money into the till. After hours you may use whatever lingo you like, particularly if you're talking to Cousin Jesse here."

I nodded. "Jamie's always had an instinct for politics," I said. "All the way through school, at least as long as I knew about it, he never once got his mouth washed out with soap—which is more than I can say."

"Some of us are *correct* by virtue of birth," Jamie Savage agreed. "And some of us run off into the wilderness before we even graduate school. Cuz, we've got a ton of catching up to do. I'd heard about Ace Tanner, sure enough, ever since I came West, but I never dreamed the famous gambler was my own blood."

Manzanita moved the footstool over, got the guitar, and placed it on the counter for me to inspect.

"Will it make music?" I asked.

"*Sí*, señor. It will make music. *Musica muy hermosa.*"

I had just killed four men—almost as though some terrible, malignant fate had control of me—almost as though I were being pursued by the Furies in the mythic tales. While it was true that I had virtually no choice in the matter—I was after all merely defending my own hide and of course Manzanita's as well—the sequence of events was hardly random. Poor stupid Abner Billingham thought he had a debt to repay, while the road agents merely wanted to take my money—though they might well have dispatched me afterward and raped and murdered Manzanita as well.

God put his human beings into a genuine crazy stew, that was certain. When plagues, floods, fires, earthquakes, droughts, volcanic eruptions, tidal waves, and the like weren't after us, we did pretty well on our own, what with wars, pillage, murder, torture, and the like. Whatever philosopher it was who claimed this to be the best of all possible worlds either had a damned peculiar vision of things or else was blind as your proverbial bat.

Had it truly been necessary for me to kill Juan José Raymondo Garcia? Indeed, would that very act not inevitably send Jesus Piedra out in search of me—so that another ambush or another gunfight was a foregone conclusion?

At the present rate of events, Johnny Mankiller might well set some sort of record before it was all over—though I'm sure from Beckwourth's point of view, or Kit Carson's, say, even two or three hundred might not amount to much. Who was it that slew a thousand with the jawbone of an ass? One of those biblical sorts that my pa used to talk about, I guess. . . .

Anyhow, the days began to drift by.

Manzanita and I didn't discuss the issue of getting formally married anymore. I guess both of us preferred just to let matters go as fate and circumstance would have it. We took a suite of rooms in the Coarse Gold Hotel as Mr. and Mrs. Jesse Tanner, and that was good enough. Manzanita kept her job with Cousin Jamie, and I spent a good bit of time on horseback, Berutti and I wandering about the area. In truth, I was thinking about acquiring some land—perhaps grasslands where I might raise cattle, perhaps a forested tract where I might put in a lumber mill, inasmuch as timber was nearly as valuable as gold, and a hell of a lot more scarce apparently. Word had it that ships with loads of lumber aboard set up for sale in Stockton—and that a couple of them were themselves scrapped for the timber in them, the ships being worth more as salvaged boards than as cargo vessels.

One day California would be a more or less civilized

place, and in that future world (as I imagined it) the day of the gambler would end, just as the days of the fur trappers had already passed by. Those who had earlier explored the Western Mountains were now the men who acted as guides to the bands of prairie schooners coming across. Jim Bridger and Louis Vasquez were tending a trading post not too many miles from the South Pass, which either Jed Smith or Bridger himself had discovered—a discovery that led to wagon trains heading for Oregon and California.

Was it just a matter of time until the whole damned West was filled with cities and farms and the like?

I took a trip back to Mokelumne Hill, partly to retrieve money from the bank, and picked up some scuttlebutt that Jesus Piedra had been arrested in Monterey and that he was to be hanged. Half an hour later, however, another fellow told me (on good authority) that Piedra had broken out of the stockade, with a little help from his friends, and had led a posse on a merry chase back into the Ventana Mountains, where the trail petered out completely. Oh yes, no doubt about it, Jesus Piedra was alive and well, but where—nobody knew. Possibly he and his gang of thieves had ridden south, onto the Baja Peninsula of Mexico—and if so, good riddance.

As Berutti and I made our way back to Coarse Gold, moving from one drainage to another, we occasionally came upon Indian sign—the Chowchillas, I theorized, for those boys were constantly into one sort of trouble or another, and were especially fond of thieving both cattle and horses. Since the white men shot deer, so the logic must have gone, it was acceptable for the red men to shoot horses and cows. In turn, the owners of the livestock would sometimes set out to avenge their losses, and there was an open season on outlaw Indians. Like wolves, mountain lions, and grizzlies, the Indians who resisted the ways of the Yankees were deemed predatory pests and were hunted and killed in the same fashion. In most cases lacking either horses or firearms, the red men attempted to fight back using spear and arrow, but such weapons were hardly sufficient. Avoidance of the white encampments was far more practical.

Even peaceful villages that allowed contact with the whites were often smitten with one plague or another—smallpox and consumption chief among these diseases to which the red men seemingly had no resistance.

Many of the Miwok Indians had already taken to mining, though this was an activity they could not legally enter into. But some had acquired enough English to communicate fairly well, and once they'd changed to *norteamericano* clothing, somehow they ceased to be Indians. The Miwoks were clever. It was simply a matter of finding some obliging drunk, someone too damned lazy to do his own digging. The Indians would strike a bargain: they'd find a likely place to mine, and their white benefactor would file a claim. From that point on, the white man would keep on drinking, and his red partners would bring in the nuggets and fines. The drunk gringo usually took fifty percent; but for his part, he provided the legality, the tools, and even weapons, though the law forbade selling firearms to the Indians.

Some of the red men, however, chose to continue in their traditional ways—to keep to themselves and to avoid the whites whenever possible. Chief Tenieya's band of Yosemite Indians, a branch of the Miwok, was such a group. During the summer months, they were said to migrate up-country, into the mysterious fastnesses of the High Sierra, a considerable area that was still essentially terra incognita at the time. The reason for this was simple: above a four- or five-thousand-foot elevation, the auriferous deposits played out—no more gold to be found. And the highest portions of the mountains were raw granite for the most part, where the earth had been scraped to the bone, so to speak, by mysterious forces far in the past. Some claimed Noah's flood had done the work, while others imagined that glaciers once lay heavy over the back of the range.

Where there was no gold for the taking, most of the Yankees did not venture. Wagon routes crossed the range to the north and to the south as well, of course— Beckwourth's Pass, Donner Pass, Carson Pass, Walker Pass near the southern end of the San Joaquin Valley. But what lay in between was still largely a matter of conjecture.

Back in Coarse Gold, I found myself drawn to the card table, and after a while the boys didn't want to play anymore. Yet I took in quite a bit of cash, a number of notes I didn't ever figure would be paid off, and a mining claim on the East Fork of the Chowchilla. Berutti and I would have to ride up there, see what the lay of the land was, see whether we could manage a four-bit pan or better.

Uncle Claude would be showing fairly soon, or so I presumed. It had now been nearly a month since the old Satan had gone off to see that widow woman in Monterey. Perhaps when he showed, if he did show, he'd have news of the fate of Señor Piedra.

I went on gambling, even as I continued to reflect on how matters stood between myself and my soul. Things with me and Manzanita were not as good as they had once been. I'd come to love her dearly, but she seemed now to be drifting away from me—or if that wasn't it, perhaps she was preoccupied with issues of her own. Whatever it was, she didn't confide in me, and I supposed I could begin to see the handwriting upon the wall.

The young lady was not a very good judge of men. Thus far in her young life she'd chosen a *cholo* bandido and a Yankee cardsharp who kept getting shot at and who therefore resorted to killing people. The truth of the matter was that I had no reasonable life to offer Manzanita, and I knew it well enough—not unless the leopard could change his spots, and damned soon.

Eventually every gunman's luck ran out, and after that it was Boot Hill.

But I continued to play cards. A Peruvian hothead by the name of Mendez took me on—Alonzo Mendez. After a run of bad luck, naturally, he accused me of cheating. Mendez took me quite by surprise—pulled a gun, something I should never in hell have allowed to happen.

As luck would have it, Mike Bonner entered the tavern at just that moment and ordered the Peruvian to put his gun on the table and his hands into the air. Mendez nodded, seemed about to follow the sheriff's directive, and then flung himself on the floor and began to fire at Bonner.

Johnny Mankiller leaped from his holster, and I fired two shots into Mendez's chest. He screamed out, blood welled from his mouth, and he lay dead on the floor.

I recognized the familiar chuckle as I replaced my Colt-Patterson. The six-shooter, I realized, was entirely without conscience—and so was I when I had the gun in my hand.

"That barstard didn't missed me head more than a couple of inches." Mike Bonner laughed. "By God, Jesse Tanner, this child owes ye one."

"Mike, if you hadn't come in just when you did, I'd be the one lying there in my own blood. I let my attention drift, I guess. He had the drop on me, dead certain."

Bonner dabbled the pool of blood with the toe of his boot, nodded.

"This one the town o' Coarse Gold pays for," he said.

So I'd managed to kill again—and again the whole thing was unexpected. It shouldn't have been, but it was. And that was when I knew I had to turn things around, set matters straight insofar as I was able. I had to find a way of making an honest living.

I wanted Manzanita, wanted her bad. But if that

wasn't possible, then I wanted—needed—someone like her. But first I had to be able to offer more than the aimless, drifting existence of a gambler's woman.

A "tame" Yosemite Indian named Ponwatchie, generally considered reliable enough to entrust with odd jobs about the mining camp, had become friends (after a fashion) with Manzanita. Ponwatchie assured me he'd look out for the girl, perhaps even attempt to determine if she still had living relatives among Tenieya's band, for he insisted that he had occasional contacts. He claimed to be on friendly terms with Tenieya himself, and he took pride in the fact that he was accepted both in the world of the red man and in the world of the white man.

So I paid Ponwatchie to keep an eye on Manzanita, and the Indian and I shook hands. I paid two months' rent at the hotel, got my things, and was gone before Manzanita returned from the mercantile.

With a pack mule trailing behind us, Berutti and I made our way upcountry to investigate that claim on the East Fork of the Chowchilla.

Berutti snorted as we rode along.

"You're telling me you're finished with gambling? What the devil is prospecting for gold if it's not gambling? Answer me that. Bad odds against winning, and a lot of hard work, that's how I see it. Well, boss, it's up to you. After all, it's your back that'll get broken, not mine. And no, I'm not going to pull any damned ore carts either."

Perhaps ten miles out of Coarse Gold I made camp. After three weeks of prepared food, a homemade meal over a campfire seemed a genuinely positive change.

But it wasn't the same as before.

"*Adiós, hermanita de mi alma,*" I said to the darkness. "Goodbye, little sister of my soul. . . . Find a man who's worthy of you this time."

At that moment what seemed like half a hundred coyotes began to howl—from all around me. There were probably only four or five coyotes, of course, but damned if they didn't have me surrounded.

Berutti whinnied as though in answer. I laughed out loud and then did my best to join into the chorus. I guess I wanted the wretched brush wolves to know I understood their game.

But later, as I drifted into sleep and as stars burned brightly against an immensity of sky, the image of a silver and turquoise coyote head hovered about the edge of my dreaming.

Thirteen

WHAT
HAPPENED
THAT WINTER

The people all were crazy then,
They didn't know what to do,
They sold their farms for just enough
To pay their passage through.

They bid their friends a long farewell;
Said, "Dear wife, don't you cry,
I'll send you home the yellow lumps,
A piano for to buy."

Fol-de-rol, Boys, fol-de-rol!

The poor, the old and rotten scows
Were advertised to sail
From New Orleans with passengers,
But they must pump or bail.

The ships were crowded more than full,
And some hung on behind,
And others dived off from the wharf
And swam till they were blind.

Fol-de-rol, Boys, fol-de-rol!

With rusty pork and stinking beef,
And rotten wormy bread;

And captains too that never were up
As high as the main masthead.

Then they thought and thought and thought
Of what they had been told—
Just how on God's green earth were caught
The Tommy-Knockers' lumps of gold.

Fol-de-rol, Boys, fol-de-rol!

T he claim on the Chowchilla proved to be essentially worthless, or so it seemed to my unpracticed
eye. Gold on a green table I could size up pretty
well, but gravel bars beside a drought-bitten stream
were more than I could estimate. It was clear that I
needed help—a partner—someone with whom I could
share my ignorance with regard to this new field of en-
deavor.

I gave some thought to Mokelumne Hill or Jackson,
but that neck of the woods was flatly overrun with
prospectors. The gravels were rich, and sixteen feet
square constituted a fair claim in places. As I saw matters, a claim of that size was hardly big enough to turn
around on. If I was setting out to mine, I wanted to do
it somewhere the boys hadn't got to yet. The Sierra
Nevada were a damned big range of mountains, so I
reasoned, and there had to be somewhere. . . .

I made my way over to the town of Mariposa, and
there I caught wind of a highly interesting rumor—
only I guess it was more than a damned rumor. Zach
Taylor had died of the cholera, and so now Millard
Fillmore was president of the United States of America.
That news didn't really affect me any, since I'd never
heard anything good about either one of those political
sonsofbitches. But the other news I picked up on was
a lot more interesting and had real implications, if you

know what I mean. California had been admitted to the Union, by God—and as a free state. I knew that some of the boys had been hoping all along for a separate country of their own, but I guessed statehood was the best thing that could have happened.

Another bit of news or rumor had a more real and immediate meaning for me, however, since it concerned some new strikes on Stanislaus River. I told Berutti what I'd heard, and he nodded as if to indicate that the place was worth taking a look at, though he didn't actually put it into those exact words, you understand. In any case, I rode north to Columbia and then down to the river and from thence upstream. A great many miners had already laid claim and were working their various portions of canyon bottom, some as I gathered with good success, others with none at all. In any case, the lads were shoveling gravel, diverting portions of the river, using cradle rocker boxes, picking away, or squatting streamside, making love to frying pans and honest-to-golly gold pans, if they'd been fortunate enough to acquire them. One old fellow with a beard as long as my arm (or almost) had a gang of Miwok Indians working for him, and they'd set up tom and riffle boxes and were shoveling gravel into the upper ends of the getups, thus allowing a flow of water to wash out the sand and mud, leaving tiny bits of the heavier gold, along with pebbles and black sand. Whatever actual nuggets might have been in the gravel bars to begin with had mostly been harvested right away—just as James Marshall had in the beginning, at Coloma. Poor Marshall, as the stories went, had no good luck since that one fateful day.

Despite the ever-present stories about California gold, in most cases it wasn't just lying there waiting to be grabbed. Your average miner, he made maybe a dollar and six bits a day, for all his work. Those river gravels broke the hearts of many a stout lad, while others gave up in disgust, sold their claims after salting them with whatever small nuggets they'd been able to collect, and then took to the byways, having first invested in a fast horse and a pair of revolvers. Let others do the picking and panning, so they concluded. With some sort of mask in place, or with none if they were brazen—like those three damn fools who came after me and Manzanita on our way to Coarse Gold—they'd attempt to relieve honest miners (or gamblers) of their hard-earned fortunes. Fellows like Jesus Piedra and Joaquin Murieta, on the other hand, they played the game from both sides—gambling when it suited them, filching when it didn't. Joaquin, he'd played more than once there at Hostetler's in Mokelumne Hill (where I'd first seen Manzanita), though I never met the man—and never saw his pickled head on display neither. But all that hadn't even happened as yet.

In truth, you know, there's magic in the word *gold* and always has been, I reckon, from the time of the ancient Egyptians to the present. There's a fever in the earth, as one fellow puts it—a kind of disease that causes otherwise rational folks to go wacky.

Intuition told me to wander on into the considerable canyon of the Middle Fork, and there I discovered, for whatever reasons, that there were fewer miners, fewer claims. Those fellas I talked to along the way all seemed basically out of sorts and ready to shuck the whole thing. There was plenty of fool's gold, and lots of black sand, but the real thing was hard to come by. In the meanwhile, the boys worked up to their asses in cold water for most of the day, digging and panning and not making a great deal. North on the Yuba, so word had it, the lads were picking up one- and two-pound nuggets, and the goose was hanging high. But here, why, that was a different matter.

Those already at work advised me to head north, but I took note that none of them seemed interested in taking his own advice. Besides, I myself had begun to hear the word *goldgoldgold* in the soughing of wind through the pines and firs. I'm not quite sure how I caught the damned disease, but that I had it now was certain. The longer I thought about things, the more I convinced myself that I never had wanted to gamble, not across a table, with dice or cards. No sir, I'd listened to Uncle Claude because, down deep, something back in those canyons of the California Sierra Nevada was calling me, even if I didn't know it and wouldn't know it for half a lifetime.

In any case, Berutti and I found our way back into the big canyon, and there I discovered a lovely little spit of land above the south bank of the stream, and above that was a deposit of red-orange sand and white gravel, back from the river, along a creek that came angling from the plateau above, in a series of cascades. The material looked remarkably similar to what was being mined back down the river, and so I set to work testing the formation.

I was a novice with a pan, of course, but I understood the basic concept of separation by weight with the assistance of swirling water. In point of fact, I didn't require very long to get the hang of it. And sonofabitch! There in the leavings, amidst black grains of metallic sand, were half a dozen pea-sized lumps of gold.

My breath came short. I could barely believe my own eyes. It made no difference that I'd routinely taken pots worth many times the amount those bits of gold represented; this was magic. Could it be that I'd actually found me a lode?

I tried pans from several different locations in the formation, and the results were virtually the same. I'd discovered a gold mine, no question about it. It might play out after a few yards of gravel, or it might. . . .

My hands were actually shaking. I was as nervous as a boy getting up the nerve to ask his girl for a first kiss—and that's just what it felt like too.

After some reflection, and after telling Berutti all about how the stick floated, I posted my claim in an empty whiskey bottle that I tied to the bole of a young ponderosa pine, made a map of the spot, and set my corners.

By bringing a flume from the top of one of the cascades, I perceived that I could create water pressure, maybe even enough to wash away at the gravel deposits that must have been left by the river at some distant point in time, perhaps before the Stanislaus had cut its canyon quite so deeply—if that's how the great God of these western mountains formed His canyons. But that was a matter for the philosophers and scientists to worry about.

Then I headed back to Columbia to see the assayer and thus to make absogoddamnlutely certain what I had was gold (which it was), and then to register a legally proper filing. Whatever I'd found, I mean however rich it might ultimately prove to be, I didn't want to lose it for want of official paperwork. Once posted, the claim was my own—to work or to sell, to break my back or to make a fortune—or something in between.

That errand done, I found my way—perhaps out of a habit that was going to be damned difficult to break—to one of the taverns, Murphy's place, where I supposed I might play a few hands of friendly blackjack or seven-card stud or have a session with the faro spread, provided I could see that the dealer was, as we say in the trade, an amateur. I was still engaged in surveying the situation in Murphy's Saloon when a familiar though unexpected voice came to me.

"Hold on thar, Jesse me lad, you're supposed to be in Coarse Gold, sure enough. Hell, I was jest on my way over thar to find ye."

It was Claudius Pennyworth McCool, none other. This time around I wouldn't have to wait for fifteen years.

"The month was past, you reprobate," I said, "so I set out to find my fortune. Truth is, I figured the señoritas of Monterey had taken your measure—put you in a coffin, by God, and planted you."

"I'll outlive ye at least ten year. How many times do I have to tell ye that? Now listen here, Jesse. Things have changed for Claude McCool. I got responsibilities now."

McCool nodded to the bartender, who brought a bottle and a pair of shot glasses for us.

"I only come looking for ye," Uncle Claude continued, "because I knew you couldn't get by without me. Whar's Manzanita? Surely ye ain't run her off, have ye?"

"Working for my cousin Jamie—and well shed of Ace Tanner, without doubt. No woman in her right mind teams with a card thief or a man who tosses disks into the mouth of El Sapo. Now what's this about responsibilities?"

"Jesse my boy, yore lookin' at an honest-to-Gawd bridegroom. My Monterey widow woman's rich, an' she wouldn't have it no other way. Well, I put up with being housebound for a spell, but then I jest had to get out o' thar, though I expect I'll go back after a bit. I rode on to San Francisco and had a leetle affair with Bella Union—that's a gambling palace, in case ye ain't been there. When I'd had my fill of faro, monte, and roulette—and had a fair stake, ye see—I put near all of it on a big-ass griz the boys had goin' against an even bigger bull from Vallejo's rancho. Turns out the griz won, jest like I thought he would. That b'ar was Gawd's own animal. Afterward we took a vote an' turned the b'ar loose, though Señor Vallejo, he didn't think much of the idea. We outvoted him, an' he said he'd try to get used to the *norteamericano* way of settling issues. The bruin took off for the hills, an' we had us a barbecue of longhorn an' a good bit of usquebaugh for the next couple of days. I spent half my take entertaining the lads, an' then I come lookin' for ye, Jesse. For the moment, this child's happy to be a free man once more. I tell ye, that marriage thing plumb restricts a feller."

"Congratulations, old man." I laughed. "You telling

me the truth, Claude? I've staked a damned gold claim upriver. Look, I'm going to work it for a time. I've got a strong hunch. You know how that goes."

"Mining? By the blue balls o' Jesus, Jesse, I swear ye've gone around the bend. Mining, is it? Well, ancient and arthritic though I be, I'll put in with ye. When I gets tired of it, I'll jest head back to Maybelle—Maybelle Rosario, that's her name, though technically it's Maybelle Magdalena Rosario McCool, like I was telling ye, since we got officially hitched. In the meantime, I'll be your damned cook, at least, an' protect ye from Injuns as well. If you don't want to card-thief no more, I guess that's yore business, though I see it as a great waste. You've got natural talent, lad. Always did have. For Claude McCool, however, it's different. I'll work weeks, but on weekends this child's going to gamble. Whar's the hole? Let's get to diggin'. You tell me thar's gold out in the canyon, and by golly we'll find 'er."

Just then a couple of shots rang out, and big Frenchy from Hangtown (as determined later) was lying there on the saloon floor, bleeding to death. The dung-squasher who gunned him down proceeded to fire off a couple of additional shots for effect, but without hitting anybody, and then he disappeared through the Dutch doors at the front of the tent-topped structure.

The boys elected not to go after the murderer inasmuch as nobody liked the Frenchman in the first place. That's pretty much how things were in California in those days.

Claude and I, we decided to get our grub and equipment together and head for the Stanislaus.

And that's how we spent the winter. For myself, I seldom left the claim for fear of getting jumped. Possession, as they say, is nine-tenths of the law. Claude, he went into town upon occasion, fetched supplies for us, and gambled a bit. He claimed he was trying to quit the habit too, but he was going at it more gradually.

It really was a hell of a winter, actually—and maybe that's my way of saying that nothing much of significance happened for the next several months—except, of course, that Claude and I struck it rich, richer than hell. My original placer kept us going quite nicely, and then, upstream along the river, around the base of a tumble of big granite boulders that made a perfect catch basin, we struck it rich a second time. Once we began to work that area, we found so many good-sized nuggets that we were tempted to ignore the fines altogether. We didn't do that, of course, but we pretended between ourselves that we ought to do it.

I saw Manzanita a couple of times—but that was before the first of the year. She was still working for Jamie, and I realized my cousin had taken a real shine to her. For her part, she was friendly but managed to keep him at a distance. And at nights she was singing and playing her guitar at Thompson's Watering Hole. For whatever reasons, the boys seemed to like her version of some Gregorian chants she'd learned at the mission and which she'd kind of adjusted around for a single voice accompanied with *la guitarra*. From what she told me, the miners would shout "Praise be the Lord!" and go on drinking. I guess Thompson's had become a kind of unofficial Church of the Holy Nugget, and Manzanita Huerfano had become their priestess, a kind of substitute Holy Virgin.

Well, I could see their point, all right. After all, I was in love with the Little Apple myself.

Once we even spent the night together. At first we just saw it as a matter of convenience. I was still paying the rent at the hotel, and she was still staying there as Mrs. Jesse Tanner, and so. . . .

It was a short time, altogether too short, a single pebble tossed into a running stream, so to put it. But the whole issue of our separation was forgotten, and we were crazy in love again, just as we had been out on the trail, and all the ache and loss and desire in my being came pouring over me until, after we had made love and she was lying there, sleeping, and looking it seemed to me like a beautiful fallen angel, I was smitten with heartache—because I knew in my bones that it wasn't time yet and maybe never would be time for the two of us.

When morning came, she knew I had to go, and accepted that. She kept smiling, but at the same time I could see a terrible sadness in her eyes, almost as though she figured we were saying good-bye for the last time. And I guess I felt the same way.

I could hear the card tables calling to me—like those sirens in Homer's *Odyssey*. It had been a right long time since I'd read that book, and I resolved that I'd have to do it again, soon, though where a fellow might find a copy in the California goldfields, I wasn't certain. I knew I wasn't going to find one on the Stanislaus. But I had enough voices in my head to do me just fine, what with Claude and Berutti and Johnny M. all ragging at me from time to time.

As to gambling, why, Claude and Oppy would head for the settlements on Friday night, like I said, and often my mentor wouldn't return until Monday night or even Tuesday, depending on whether the streak he was riding at the moment was for winning or for losing.

The winter months came, and with them rain— sometimes rain for a week or two at a time. At year's end we began to see snow along the canyon's rim, and in February the white stuff found its way down to us. The river was running so high at that time that I was half afraid we wouldn't have any gravel deposits left next to those granite boulders when the flood backed off. What I'm saying is that our mining activities got put to the rear of the stove, so to speak, until the weather decided to cooperate.

The really bad spells didn't last too long, after all.

The framed tent we put up kept dry most of the time, and the canvas didn't even rip through in the aftermath of one heavy snowstorm that turned the entire canyon into a white desert.

Except for the few days when our creek was frozen damned near solid, we kept washing sand and gravel, and by the time the good weather came again—with redbud and wild mock orange and lupines and poppies shouting their colors from the grassy areas below us and from the slopes above, at about the time when the mockingbirds started singing their heads off half the night long—by then we had several pokes full of gold: nuggets and dust to the tune of about twenty thousand dollars, as we calculated the matter, though as it turned out, we were being overly conservative in our estimate. With an accurate weigh-in, we were closer to thirty thousand.

"McCool," I said casually, "we're rich men, or soon will be. Even at your advanced age, that's got to mean something."

"Indeed it does, lad. But I don't figger I ought to stay much longer. Maybelle, she's going to be powerful annoyed with me as is. Hell, maybe she figgers I'm dead or summat, and has up and married all over again. I'd be powerful disappointed, if that were the case. I'm genuinely fond of that lady, Jesse."

For myself, I was thinking of Manzanita Huerfano, and I said as much.

"Left 'er with your cousin, did ye? Well, I figger ye ought to go check things out. Mebbe she'll have ye back, who knows? Well, ye've got a gold mine, sure enough, and a proven one too. But this child thinks it makes more sense and is more civilized to let other dumb bastards dig the gold and then fetch it from them with playing cards. I figure I can quadruple my share o' the winter's earnings in a couple of weeks. The cards work better when a fellow's got a genuine stash to operate with, as ye know. Don't guess as I want to do any more of that mining, Jesse. When a man gets to be middle-aged, like me, that kind of work wears him down."

I laughed. "Middle-aged, my English ass. Claude, you'd complain if you were hanged with a new rope, for God's sake. Mr. McCool, that hillside's full of gold—I can feel it in my bones. And furthermore, you're the oldest man in the world, or close to it."

Claude laughed. "Ain't neither. Maybelle, she said I was as randy as any sixteen year old."

"And how would Maybelle know about that?" I asked.

"Just common sense, lad. Common sense. Ye headin' to Coarse Gold? Let's buy each other a drink or two first and see if Lady Luck's on our side."

"Gray-bearded Satan." I whistled. "Get thee behind me. The whole reason I went to gold mining was to put that kind of life out of mind. We're well on to being rich men, and it's all as a result of honest work."

McCool chuckled. "I been holding down two jobs this winter, Jesse, and ye didn't even know it. To tell the truth, I kind of invested that roll I won on the grizzly bear, and the whole thing sort of compounded. Since we was partners, I guess I owe you half of what I made on weekends, just like I got half of what ye panned out while I was gone them days. Point of fact, I've accumulated about twenty thousand on my own. Ten of it's yours. That way we've got near twenty-five apiece. Claudius McCool, he's going to make tracks for Monterey, if Oppy's still got that many miles left in 'im."

"You *are* coming back, I take it?"

Claude took off his hat and rubbed at his scar. He winked and spat tobacco juice as we rode along.

"When a coon gets middle-aged," he said, "it don't make much sense to plan things out. We all owe the Big Cahuna a death, an' that's one debt there's no way of chiseling on. A man can't jest ride out of town, if you catch my drift. But I've made 'er this far, and so likely ye'll see me again."

At Murphy's Tavern we ordered a bottle and two shot glasses, tossed off a few, fed a few coins to El Sapo without winning, and talked for a spell about the days back in Pennsylvania, when I was just a kid.

McCool said he was intending to use the gentlemen's room and would be right back.

Only he wasn't. The old card player just walked on out at the other end of the latrine, mounted Oppy, and rode toward Monterey.

I thought about tracking him, but decided to let things stand as they were. Claude had a way of disappearing and then showing up when a man least expected him.

For myself, I was on my way to Coarse Gold. With a small but honestly earned fortune in my saddlebags, I was ready to start in on a new life. Would Manzanita appreciate my medicine vision, so to speak? Would she be willing to share a log-framed tent house for a season or two? Or had she found another friend in my absence?

If that were true, of course, I could hardly have blamed her.

Fourteen

WHAT HAPPENED TO MANZANITA

And anywhere you went to work,
A fortune could be made, sir,
With nothing but a rocker, pan,
A bucket, or a spade, sir.
And sometimes with a butcher's knife,
You'd work a little while, sir,
And e'er you knew what you had done,
You'd made a bully pile, sir.

Whack fol de da, ri tol lol da,
Te my whack fol de da!

If one was found a rascal then,
Men took his case in hand, sir,
And made him go to pulling hemp,
Or drove him from the land, sir.
But men are more enlightened now,
And stringent laws will make, sir,
And officers enforce the same,
To raise a poker stake, sir.

Whack fol de da, ri tol lol da,
Te my whack fol de da!

But now, alas! Those times have flown,
We ne'er shall see them more, sir.

But let us do the best we can,
And dig for golden ore, sir.
And if we strike a decent lead,
Let's work and not repine, sir,
But take things easy as they did
In good old 'Forty-Nine, sir.

Whack fol de da, ri tol lol da,
Te my whack fol de da!

With Uncle Claude having once again disappeared into the woodwork, as the saying goes, I saddled Berutti, mounted, thrust my weight back against the cantle, rattled the jinglebobs on my spurs, thrust the toes of my boots into the tapederos, and used my knees to urge my faithful stallion into motion.

"Where we headed, boss?"

"Coarse Gold, naturally enough," I replied, glancing about to assure myself no one there on the main street of town was listening to me.

Berutti shook his head, fluttered his lips, and then gritted his teeth.

"Naturally enough. Madame Manzanita. So I get to see little Deuce again, eh? I bet she'd throw a mean foal if you'd just give me the opportunity to get her into a family way."

"Never can tell," I said. "Let's hit the trail."

With more than usual enthusiasm, so it seemed to me, Berutti trotted along the main thoroughfare of Mariposa, the place of butterflies. Matter of fact, he damned near jolted me out of the saddle, and I cursed under my breath.

Johnny Mankiller was firmly strapped to my waist again, something of an odd sensation after going gunless for most of the winter. I don't mean that I didn't keep my *pistola* close at hand, you understand, but working with mud and water that way, a pistol is easily corroded. Sand gets into the mechanism, and so forth. Mostly I kept my gun belt cinched about one of the alders that grew beside my creek.

Now, with the money I'd earned honestly, and with the further amounts of lead that were sure to come out of my claim, I might well be able to offer Manzanita Huerfano the type of life she deserved. Of course, there was always the possibility that she'd forgotten all about Ace Tanner. Hell, she might already be married, for all I knew. A beautiful single girl in a mining town, a señorita who could play the guitar, sing, recite Latin poetry if she had to . . . Well, she'd have been a prize catch, no matter what.

Spring was in full flower at this point—if anything, just past its prime. Leaves were already out on the black oaks and were just coming on the blue oaks that studded the lower hills. Poppies and lupines were everywhere, and even the wild lilac was splatched in white flames all over the hills. Little golden tulips with fuzzy throats, snakeheads, larkspurs, and wood violets were everywhere, and in the creek bottoms the fanworts were up, their slender stalks bearing crowns of pink flowers. The manzanita brush continued to stutter the last of its tiny white bells, but in the yellow pine and hemlock-fir belt it was still blooming. In a couple more weeks, the azaleas along the canyon bottoms would be in flower, they with their delicate, molasses-honey odor.

When I was a boy, if I may digress for just a moment, I had a genuine fondness for wildflowers, and was eager to know their names. Pa always believed I was wasting my time, but the lady who taught school was impressed with my collections of pressed blossoms. What the devil was her name? Memory's a strange pack of cards.

Miss Malone. I don't know why you can't remember something as simple as that.

It pleased me to think of my teacher. In point of fact, I hadn't thought of her in quite a long while. A recent graduate of normal school, she was young and pretty, and if ever a six-year-old boy was in love with a mysterious older woman, why that was me—if you get my drift. Amidst all this springtime glory, I rode into Coarse Gold.

Manzanita Huerfano, however, was not at James Savage's trading post when I arrived. In point of fact, she hadn't been there for some time.

Cousin Jamie shook my hand perhaps three or four times—and three or four times told me that I was looking good, healthy as your basic Pennsylvania hog.

"I wanted to get word to you, Jesse," he said, "and I even sent messages out to Sonora and Angels Camp and Mokelumne Hill and a few other places, hoping someone had seen you and could make contact. Hell, man, for all I knew, you'd headed back to Oregon country."

Jamie, as I could see, was being altogether too damned apologetic. He was still pumping my hand all the while he was telling me this.

"But surely you know where she is? I imagine I'll want to track her down. We've got a little bit of unfinished business, and—"

"Tell you what, Jess. Here's the story, blunt and simple. The Little Apple has run off to live with Tenieya's Yosemite Injuns, and Ponwatchie doesn't know beans about it. I think the man's telling the truth. I've never had any reason to doubt his word. Honest as the day is long. With Injuns, a man can always tell. You ain't going to like what comes next, cousin. I've heard of your run-ins with Jesus Piedra—Manzanita told me the whole damned story, in glowing detail. She's in love with you—and was heartbroken when you disappeared last autumn. Well, Piedra showed up here in Coarse Gold. Word gets around, and he heard that you and

Manzanita were living together. California's a big place, but not when it comes to gossip. News spreads."

"Come on, Jamie, get to the point. What happened, for God's sake?"

James Savage checked the hour on his fob watch and then withdrew a handkerchief, blew his nose. He was, I realized, stalling for time—like a man who has to say something but doesn't quite know how to do it.

"Three nights in a row Piedra come to Thompson's Watering Hole, and the third time is when it happened—afterward, I mean, with her on the way back to the hotel. What I'm saying, Jesse, is that he beat hell out of her and raped her. That's what she told Mike Bonner the next day—beat the dickens out of her and forced himself on her, or at least tried to. Well, she didn't actually say so—but she was bruised around the mouth and eyes. Muddy Mike, he arrested Jesus right away and tried to wrestle a confession out of him, but it didn't do any good. I think Mike probably pistol-whipped the *cholo* sonofabitch pretty good. You know how Mike is. He's got a real bad temper when it comes to someone thumping on a lady. But finally Piedra got him a lawyer, you see, and so Bonner didn't have any choice except to set him free and tell him to get the hell out of town—since Manzanita had already disappeared, went off with Ponwatchie's help—at least that's what we all figured at the time. The bastard's back now—Piedra, I mean—that's what I hear. He was playing cards at Thompson's Watering Hole just last night. Goddamn it, Jesse Tanner, I know what you're thinking, but you've got to use your head."

I drummed my fingers on the table.

"Bonner'd put Piedra in the hooskow if he could, but if Jesus Piedra's actually wanted by the law, no one north of the Tehachapis seems to know or care about it. No warrant, no arrest. And that's the name of the game. You're good with the gun, all right—I know that, and so does everybody else, including Piedra. You've got a reputation. Could be he did the job on

Manzanita primarily to smoke you out, you know, force you into a showdown. But if you're going after Piedra, it's got to be a fair fight—and he's got to be the one who starts it. Otherwise, Muddy Mike'll have to put your tail feathers into the jail, and when the miners get soused on a Saturday night, they're likely to string up anybody Mike's got in custody. The pope's grandmother wouldn't be safe when the boys are out to have a good time."

I continued to drum my fingers.

"Look, let's give it a couple of days. Piedra's after Manzanita again—he's been asking questions. The militia—kind of a vigilance committee, so to speak—I guess we'll take care of Señor Piedra soon enough. You stay out of it, Jesse Tanner."

"Folks call me Ace," I replied, patting the handle on my Colt-Patterson.

Johnny Mankiller, he was starting to growl.

There was another and possibly far more serious problem, however, for it was also rumored that Manzanita Huerfano had become a renegade, acting as a conduit and supplying arms to the Indians. Besides that, at least one stage holdup was attributed to her, and under the circumstances, I wouldn't put it past her, that's certain. She'd doubtless been with Piedra himself more than once on just such a venture, and she could see as well as any fool just how those three road agents made their mistakes when they tried to take us.

I talked to Muddy Mike, who just shook his head and said it was too damned bad I took so long in getting on back to Coarse Gold. Most likely he was right.

In any case, the Brannen and Johnson stage line had posted a five-hundred-dollar reward for her scalp—on pure suspicion.

The vigilance committee was backing the stage line—and my cousin was a major in the volunteer militia, and that group was pretty much the same as the vigilance committee itself, when you got right down to it.

"My own post has been raided by the damned Yosemites," Jamie said. "And who'd know better about the routines and so forth than Manzanita? Even so, I wouldn't let the bounty hunters for Brannen and Johnson put up the damned poster outside my store. Didn't seem right, somehow, even if she's guilty as sin. Jesse, it just figures, that's all. I wish it was different, but it ain't, and there's not much either of us can do about it. One of my own men got put under, his throat slit. That's murder and a whole lot more. It may be our fault that Manzanita's gone bad—for not protecting her, I mean. But that don't change anything. Once a person takes that trail down the mountain, man or woman, white man or red man, there's no going back. The fat's in the fire whether we want it to be or not."

Sick at heart, I nodded. What Jamie said made a great deal of sense. It figured. It looked like it ought to pan out.

When I walked over to the bank, there was the wanted poster, printed fancy as hell. I tell you, it made my heart sick all over again just to see the thing.

WANTED, REWARD, $500 FOR THE SCALP OF MANZANITA HUERFANO. WE DON'T CARE WHAT YOU DO WITH HER AFTER YOU APPREHEND HER. WE JUST WANT THE SCALP AND SOME KIND OF PROOF IT CAME FROM HER. NO QUESTIONS ASKED.

I studied the wording. Nice fellas. Damned nice.

The evidence was a long way from being solid, though, and in fact it wasn't even solidly circumstantial; and yet everybody in town seemed certain it was so. Tenieya's Yosemite Miwoks were responsible, and the most compelling proof was that the best efforts to determine their location had gone for nothing. Tenieya and his wretched Yosemites had just by-God disappeared, back into the unmapped Sierra Nevada, most likely. Some figured the Indians had gone south to the

Kings or to the San Joaquin, while a few others suggested the Stanislaus or the Merced.

Years back I had the good fortune of meeting that fellow named Zenas Leonard, a man who had actually come across the Sierra Nevada in 1833, the year when all the stars fell from their places, as the Hopi Indians put it. Leonard, he had been a kind of recording clerk for the expedition Bonneville sent out, that one with Joe Meek and Joe Walker both, with Meek had his company crossing the range to the north, while Walker and his bunch went south and damned near died in the snow. Leonard told me about the mountains, and even if I wasn't especially interested at the time, it did my heart good just to hear the man talk. You'd have thought he was living the whole thing over again. Then he showed me his journal, all carefully written in that kind of precise hand that some folks have, even if I don't. While I can't remember the words exactly, they went something like this:

We traveled a few miles every day, still on the top of the mountain, and our course continually obstructed with snow hills and rocks. Here we began to encounter in our path, many small streams which would shoot out from under these snow banks, and after running a short distance in deep chasms which they have through ages cut in the rocks, precipitate themselves from one lofty precipice to another, until they are exhausted in rain below. Some of these precipices appeared to us to be more than a mile high. Some of the men thought that if we could succeed in descending one of these precipices to the bottom, we might thus work our way into the valley below—but on making several attempts we found it utterly impossible for a man to descend, to say nothing of our horses.

In two or three days we arrived at the brink of the mountain. This at first was a happy sight, but when we approached close, it seemed to be so near perpendicular that it would be folly to attempt a descent. In looking on the plain below with the naked eye, you have

one of the most singular prospects in nature; from the
great height of the mountain the plain presents a dim
yellow appearance—but on taking a view with the spy
glass we found it to be a beautiful plain stretched out
towards the west until the horizon presents a barrier to
the sight. From the spot where we stood to the plain
beneath, must at least be a distance of three miles, as
it is almost perpendicular, a person cannot look down
without feeling as if he was wafted to and fro in the
air, from the giddy height.

Was it to such a place that Manzanita had retreated?

I knew very well that I was either going to have to
get back to the claim on the Stanislaus or send a crew
of some kind, or just forget about the whole thing.
Under the circumstances, I concluded, there was too
much at stake just to walk away—in the fashion of the
old Ace Tanner. Truth is, I'd walked away from a great
many good things in my life.

I got hold of Ponwatchie, of course, right away—to
see what I could discover about Manzanita's whereabouts. Whatever the man had told or not told the
others, he was straight with me—and loyal enough,
since he'd been in my employ all along, a bit of information I hadn't even shared with Cousin Jamie.

"She's with Tenieya, then?" I asserted more than
asked.

"Yep. I went with her to Merced River. We camped
there and kept a fire going. Some of us have come to
live among the Owl-faces and have jobs—earn good
money, like me. But we wear the white man's clothing,
and after that we begin to look like Owl-faces ourselves. That's why we all promise Tenieya and the
council that we will never come back to the secret
place. Too dangerous. Like right now. Them damn
Chowchillas rob a stagecoach and kill the driver, then
the whites blame Yosemites and want to take Manzanita's scalp. No point telling them guys nothing. I even
said to Muddy Mike it was the Chowchillas, but he

don't listen either. He just hears what the miners say, and they twist things around for no reason at all. But me, there's some things I don't tell, no matter what. If Jamie Savage finds out where Tenieya takes the people, then that militia he commands will want to go there and kill everybody."

I grinned, thumped Ponwatchie on the back, and winked at him.

"You're a good man, my friend," I said. "And you've been around the whites, the *Saldu*, long enough to know how their minds work."

Ponwatchie nodded.

"Yes," he said, "the Saldu. Your people have law, Ace Tanner, but sometimes that law does not work right. I am Miwok, and yet I live among your people. I know them, and they trust me. I work for them, and I work honestly. I do not wish to accept pay for work I have not done. I know that I must walk straight, or the law will be turned against me. For the Saldu themselves, there is a longer riata, a longer chain made of rope. Muddy Mike Bonner enforces the law—at least that part of the law he knows about. But there is so much law—it must fill many books."

"I understand," I replied. "For myself, I don't trust those Mariposa Militia boys a bit. They've strung up more than one coon dawg, only to find out later they had the wrong fellow. No point in apologizing after a hanging, though, is there? But I need to find Manzanita—you understand, my friend? I want her to be my wife—if she'll have me, that is."

Ponwatchie grinned. "Damned fool Saldu for leaving her behind, then. Good-looking woman like that, half the men in Coarse Gold want her to take off her clothes. But she was waiting for you, I think."

"You can't take me to Tenieya—I understand that. But will you go there yourself—take a message for me? Perhaps the Little Apple will be willing to meet me somewhere. Whatever else has happened, she knows she can trust me."

Ponwatchie rubbed at his nose and chin, then adjusted the battered stovepipe hat he was in the habit of wearing. I guess it was a kind of symbol for him, a mark of his being accepted, after a fashion, into the world of the mines. At a distance, in fact, a man could hardly tell him from one of the local rowdies.

"You been straight with me, Ace Tanner. And Manzanita, she's got eyes for you. So maybe I will take you there if you wish, just as I did with her. I build a fire and wait for Tenieya's scouts to find us. After that, they decide what to do."

Secret place. Somewhere like Hidalgo Village perhaps—a hunting encampment possibly, in some high meadow where the snow melts out early—or maybe some hot springs, a place where the animals winter and thus provide food for a small group of Yosemite Indians. Or maybe the place that Zenas Leonard described in his journal . . .

"The hideout," I said, glancing away from Ponwatchie, "it's back in a valley surrounded by cliffs, a place where there are waterfalls. Am I right?"

I turned to him then and met his eyes. He stared back without blinking. I tell you, that Indian would have made a hell of a poker player—and indeed I'd heard some of the fellows say that he'd fleeced them at the stick game. Well, one should never wrestle another kid in that kid's own front yard. So Ponwatchie stared at me, his face utterly devoid of expression.

"When you want to go Merced River?" he asked.

That night someone set the Blood & Sweat Saloon on fire, and the makeshift structure quickly burned to the ground, taking with it a building or two adjacent on either side. The hour was close to midnight, and I'd already made preparations to retire for the night. The truth of the matter was that I was feeling sorry for myself, more than a little angry at the world, and half in the mood to settle in for one last binge at a card table.

I mean, hell, a fella can't just quit cold turkey, can he?

I could see the fire out of my window, and so I put my jacket back on and, almost as an afterthought, strapped on Johnny Mankiller. Taking one last snort from the whiskey bottle, I closed the door behind me and strode down the stairway to the nearly empty anteroom below.

"Fire," the night clerk said, gesturing in such a way that no further question was admissible.

I nodded and walked out into the night, ambled the three blocks to where the Blood & Sweat had once stood—and where portions of it still stood, burning.

A hell of a little bonfire, actually. . . .

Mike Bonner himself was on the water wagon, attempting, over all the uproar, to direct the two men with hoses to be more sparing with the water and the boys who were manipulating the gear pump to keep up the pressure.

It was already a lost cause.

"The work o' those damned Yosemites!" a heavyset individual yelled out. "Ought to lynch the lot o' them!"

"Have to find them red Arabs first," another put in. "The devil's own children, they are. What do ye say, mate?"

"Shit," another man bawled, "it weren't Injuns at all. One o' the hoors got drunk and knocked over a lantern, that's all."

"Which one was it, Jake? We'll string 'er up, by Gawd!"

"Keep that pump going," Bonner shouted, "or by God's green ding-dong, I'll lynch the lot of ye!"

At that point one of the first men of the city of Coarse Gold, a man by the name of Lafayette Bunnell, climbed alongside Mike Bonner and thereafter took over the task of telling the volunteer firemen and those in the bucket brigade what to do.

Standing there, watching and listening, I knew as

certain as anything on earth that it was just a matter of
time before James Savage and his volunteer militiamen
would set out to track the wily Yosemites. No matter
how big a range the Sierra might be, ultimately there'd
be nowhere to hide. Once Yankees get determined,
there's no stopping them. When that happened, a few
of Tenieya's men would likely be hanged, and the rest
of the band would be sent over to a rancheria in the
Coast Range, to land where nobody had ever found
any gold. To put Indians on rancherias in the midst of
an area where any given acre of ground could well
turn out to be the bonanza itself, why hell, that just
didn't make any sense to anyone. In the meanwhile,
the Chowchillas—if indeed it was them—would continue their merry ways.

One particular whore, in the aftermath of the fire,
would find it the better part of valor to keep her pretty
little mouth shut about what really happened there in
the Blood & Sweat Saloon.

When the boys came back from lynching Tenieya
and his cronies, they'd likely be in a mood for spend-
ing. In any case, it wouldn't take all that long to rig
another tent frame for the Blood & Sweat II.

Since it was beginning to look as though the Coarse
Gold Water Company would indeed manage to get the
fire under control before it burned down the entire settlement, I turned to walk back to my hotel room.

That's when I saw him, standing back in the shadows—there, and then gone—Jesus Piedra.

Johnny Mankiller was humming softly once again.

"Patience, Jonathan," I cajoled. "Patience, my little
friend."

Fifteen

JOHNNY MANKILLER SPEAKS HIS PIECE

I am going to California
As sure as I am born,
And I wonder if I'd better go
A-sailing 'round the Horn
Or had better go by Panama,
The old and beaten way
And see the towers and castles old
With walls so grim and gray.

I think I'll go the other way;
In Ephraim Jones' letter
He says the Nicaragua route
Than the other two is better.
So I'll take a ship some pleasant day,
And sail across the sea,
To find the monster Elephant,
Wherever he may be.

I wonder how the critter looks
And if he doesn't stand
With hind feet on the waters
And fore feet on the land.
Eph says I'll see him, tusks and all

Before I reach the diggin's
With the long tom lashed upon his back
And all a miner's riggin's.

I went to the livery to take care of my good friend
Berutti—to give him his grain and a few well-placed
stokes with a curry comb, put on his favorite saddle
blanket, and cinched on the slick fork saddle and saddlebags. The horse eyed me suspiciously but said nothing. Nonetheless, I could tell that he was, as the
children say, bored. He was ready for out next adventure, and now he was certain something was about to
happen.

"You stay here awhile longer," I said. "Chances are
there'll be some lead flying this morning sometime.
Once that little matter's taken care of, we'll head off to
see if we can find Manzanita and Deuce. It may be that
you and I both have the same designs in mind, my
friend."

The stallion ignored me, nosed at his oats and barley
instead. Only when I offered him a chunk of bread
sopped in blackstrap sorghum did he seem to take any
genuine interest in his master's presence.

"Wish me luck," I said over my shoulder as I left
him. I was almost to the main door of the barn when
I detected a faint but familiar fluttering of equine lips.

"Be back this afternoon, if not sooner," I said to
One-eyed Joe, who was tending the business at the moment. If the man had been watching me from a distance, he now looked away, concentrated on something
else—as though he didn't want to be involved in chit-
chat, at least not with Ace Tanner.

"Good enough," Joe replied—without so much as
looking up from the tattered copy of the *Sacramento
Union* that he was reading. For no real reason, I found

I was surprised Joe could read, and I guessed that I'd jumped to a conclusion.

Maybe, after all, both Berutti and Joe were responding to something in me—something like the hatred that had taken hold of my insides, a bellyache, let's say, which, at the same time, suggested its own cure. Possibly I just wasn't very good company at the moment.

I walked the length of Main Street, beyond the turnoff to a scattering of diggin's along Fresno River, which was no more than a creek in this particular area, as I said once or twice before.

I stopped at the CG Bakery, bought three unleavened doughnuts that had been cooked in lard and then dipped in a honey pot—the sweetener having come from a hollow live oak, as I knew, courtesy of Ponwatchie himself. Many of the big live oaks in this region of the foothills were rotten inside, hollow, and hence perfect homesteads for the native bees. This time of year the honey tasted distinctly of manzanita—unless it was the old, heavy stuff from the previous season, in which case a fellow might think the bees had been after dung flowers. In any case, if aged, the sweet substance was gritty between a man's teeth.

Fortunately, my doughnuts tasted of manzanita flowers, and I contemplated the poetic significance of that fact. Damned good, to tell the truth.

From the bakery I proceeded to the Savage Mercantile. Cousin Jamie was off on business—taking orders for woolen goods at North Fork, or so the clerk said. Ponwatchie had been splitting firewood in Jamie's employ, fuel for the blacksmith's forge, so I left a message for my Injun pal care of Cousin Jamie, one that would make sense only to Ponwatchie:

Hekeke Osa-be, smoke where the river runs.

Ten o'clock in the morning, and the boys were just finding their way into Thompson's Watering Hole. With the Blood & Sweat temporarily out of business, the other saloons would each have a few more customers than usual.

I ordered a shot of good whiskey, tossed it off, nodded, and thumped the shot glass on the adzed surface of the big plank that sufficed as a bar. A heathen Chinee—excuse me, a Celestial—was tending the saloon. His name was Tommy Chan, and I'd played poker with him a year earlier—played to a standoff. He was a friendly chap, and I liked him a great deal—without really knowing why. Possibly it's because the Chinese are more polite than most people, more willing to think logically and fairly about things. Or maybe it was just because Chan-Tommy and I got along, simple as that.

There were race problems in California in those days, no two ways about it. Part of me even felt sorry for Jesus Piedra, the man I'd taken a vow to kill—the man who had sealed his own fate when he accosted Manzanita, though doubtless the damned fool still thought of her as his personal property. The Mexicans in particular nursed deep resentment toward the new Yankee government—since Alta California had been, until quite recently, theirs, so to speak. But of course they never had convinced the Indian tribes to go along with their schemes, despite the attempts of the padres at the missions. In any case, Indians, Mexicans, and Chinese were regarded as foreigners, and the law that worked half-ass for most of us hardly worked at all for them. The previous year the California legislature imposed a so-called "work tax" on foreign labor, and because of this nuisance law, almost no Mexicans or Chinese worked in the mining operations. With the Indians things were different. The boys who had "turned white" proceeded to find a Yank to front them and hold the claim, while they did all the work in exchange for half the profits.

So the road agents and bandidos took a living as they were able—and that included the half-dozen or so Joaquins (reputed to give money to the poor) and my dear friend Jesus Piedra as well.

"You going to kill someone, Ace Tanner? You got

that look in eyes. Better not drink no more rotgut. Don't shoot straight. Piedra, he in town?"

Chan glanced at a big mirror that had recently been installed in the Watering Hole.

"It'll be out in the street," I said in response to the unasked question.

Chan dipped my empty shot glass into a tub of soapy, gray-colored liquid, wiped the thumb-tumbler dry with a white cloth, then placed the glass back into a rack designed for that particular purpose.

"Don't want bury you, Tanner. Maybe Piedra hears you in Coarse Gold, runs away."

I shook my head. "Whatever else the man is," I said, "he's no coward, Tom. This is something that needs settling."

"What we do if Muddy Mike puts you in jail for killing Piedra? I like see hangings, but not yours."

For a brief moment I could imagine myself dangling, strung from a big branch in one of the great-limbed oaks that grew amidst the pines close to town. At first there was but a single person, dressed in black, vulturine, standing there to mourn my passing—none other than good-hearted Tommy Chan. Then a second and a third—Uncle Claude and a lady with iron-gray hair, Maybelle, presumably, the rich former widow lady from Monterey, but now Mrs. Claude McCool. So the ancient fox had finally settled down, and it was about time too. Meanwhile, off at a distance a coyote was yowling, and a vision of Manzanita's beautiful face brought me back to my senses.

"*Ven aqui, gringo*. Maybe we play poker, *sí*? What you got to bet with this time? Where you hiding my leetle *perra*? I'm talking to you, *comprende*?"

I had made a great mistake as I sat there on the bench outside the Watering Hole—I'd allowed my mind to drift to other times, other places. In fact, I was recalling a tale Manzanita had told me, not a story of her own people, but rather one she'd learned from the mission priests, of all people: an Indian tale from the Platte River country, the Arapaho. In this story a badger fooled a lovely maiden by disguising himself as a handsome young fellow who belonged to the warrior society called Foxes. The maiden brought badger a goat-horn spoon filled with soup, and he drank from it, thus accepting her as his bride-to-be. When the badger left her to go to the sun dance, however, the maiden discovered his true identity and instead married a good-looking, thirty-six-year-old gambler named Jesse Tanner.

Well, I may have changed a few of the details.

Now I looked up slowly, and the ugly face I anticipated, that of Jesus Piedra, was indeed there before me like some grotesque Navajo kachina mask.

I carefully placed both hands on my lap as I met his gaze.

"Amigo," I said, "how's the stick floating? If you're looking for Miss Huerfano, why, I haven't seen her in several months. I hear she's gone off to live among the Tenieya's band of Yosemites. I don't guess she liked you or me either one. Perhaps we should join forces to go search for her. . . ."

Piedra took a short step backward, as though to provide sufficient room for him to go for his gun and still be able to squeeze off a clean shot as I tried to get at my own weapon.

Johnny Mankiller was growling softly, happily, in his holster—as though in anticipation of his moment in the sunlight. If I were killed, I fully realized, Johnny would be pleased enough to ride on another man's hip. Perhaps, after all, it hardly mattered if a given lead slug struck its mark or didn't. Doubtless the worthless bastard would be satisfied to become Piedra's companyero, if it came to that, so long as the outlaw provided sufficient excitement.

Keep yore peace, leetle man. I've got plans for ye. . . .

The moment had come, and no time to do any more thinking. . . .

"*Chinga tu madre . . .*" Piedra was saying just as I lunged forward, driving the top of my head into his belly and sending him sprawling backward onto the wagon-rutted street.

Then I was astride him, like a mountain cat taking a deer, so to speak, or as the hungry wolf, finding no game more substantial, resorts to the burrows of mice and prowls the tufted hillsides, dancing lightly before pouncing on its prey, then crushing the furry morsel between powerful jaws—at least that's how Homer might have made the comparison in *The Iliad* or *The Odyssey*.

In any case, it did my heart good to catch Jesus the Terrible off guard and off balance that way, and within moments I was raining punches to his face and forehead.

"*Chinga! Chinga! Chinga, mierda!*" Jesus shouted.

Within a moment I realized that I'd greatly underestimated my opponent's strength. He flung me backward, and I struck the edge of the boardwalk—but was able to twist to one side just in time. Piedra lunged for me, and as he did so, I caught him with the point of my boot, not in the face as I'd hoped, but across the side of his neck. His sombrero spun off in the same motion, and was held fast only by the knotted stampede string fastened by a silver and turquoise slide piece.

I was expecting Piedra to go for his gun at this point, but strangely enough, that didn't happen. Time had slowed, as often happens during a confrontation of this sort, slowed to a virtual crawl—and consequently my vision darted about until it found what it sought. There was Piedra's weapon, ten or so feet away, lying in the street behind where he crouched, cursing, the sombrero half covering his *cholo* face.

I spun immediately, gaining my balance on one knee. As I started to rise, Piedra came at me again, this time with his Puerto Vallarta toothpick in hand, a dagger with a long, thin, curved blade, the kind often used for gutting and scaling fish, as I told you earlier.

In the curious lucidity of that moment, I could actually smell the man's breath—foul with whiskey and beans and cheese that may have been half fermented to start with and was now half digested. As though from a position of utter calm, I made note of the even, square white teeth, the waxed mustache, the brown, acne-pocked skin of the man's face. The point of my boot, I surmised, had brought my opponent nearly to regurgitation, something only fierce anger had restrained—hence the peculiar combination of odors.

Already the toothpick had begun its downward arc. Sunlight gleamed from the blade above me as I anticipated the fatal stab, the flow of my own blood. Strangely enough, I have no recollection of that interval of perhaps a second or two, and only the sound brought me back to full awareness. For Johnny Mankiller was in my hand and a rich odor of gun smoke all about me, there where I was still kneeling.

Jesus Piedra sagged to the ground even as I rose to my feet. Very calmly I proceeded to empty Johnny Mankiller's six-shot cylinder into my already dead foe. I continued, quite deliberately, until the Colt-Patterson's hammer fell with a metallic click. One of my shots, I noted, fired at nearly point-blank range, had caused Piedra's forehead to explode, possibly due to the slug's striking at an angle and thus causing the skull case to shatter. Brains oozed over the side of the man's face.

The few who were on the street this morning, still an hour and a half or more before noon, had taken cover at the sound of gunfire. But now, as I noted, first one face then a second and a third, appeared from behind the corners of buildings. A strange silence hung about the place, and I breathed deeply as I popped out the Colt-Patterson's empty cylinder and replaced it with a loaded spare that I invariably carried in my jacket pocket.

Johnny Mankiller was humming a military tune as I slid him back into his holster.

"Here! This way," Tommy Chan hissed from behind me, holding open the Dutch doors. "Through saloon, out the back. Better you get out of here quick, Ace Tanner."

I did as Chan advised, knowing good logic when I hear it, striding quickly through the building and then making my way to the livery. To One-eyed Joe's great surprise, I slapped a ten-dollar gold piece on the bench beside him, mounted the indomitable Berutti, and urged the stallion to a full run as we sped out of Coarse Gold.

If Muddy Mike takes time to think matters through, by cracky, he'll realize ye done 'im a favor. But in the meanwhile, lad, it's best to make yore presence scarce as by-Gawd hens' teeth.

"I hear you, Claude. What you're telling me hits the nail right on the nose. The Pope shits in the woods, and a bear's Catholic, by golly. It's half of one, six dozen of the other. . . ."

Naturally enough, I had the bad fortune of encountering half a dozen of Piedra's scouts as I made my way out of town. At least they looked like his bunch, and I'm almost certain I recognized one fellow—like he might have been a brother to the Juan José Raymondo Garcia I shot as Manzanita and I and Uncle Claude were on our way from Piedra's village there on the slopes of Monte Piños.

Well, I was in a hurry and in no mood to stop for a conversation, so I let Johnny Mankiller speak my piece. He was just getting into the groove again and needed practice anyhow. I could tell that was true by the tone of his Satanic chuckling. Three grinnin' fools went under as Berutti and I galloped past them. And that made four dead men in less than half an hour.

More notches for the Colt-Patterson's handle, if I chose
to cut them. At the present rate, however, Johnny Boy
wouldn't have any hickory hand pieces left before
many more moons went by.

I resolved, by Gawd, to mend my ways—but the
present moment wasn't the right time. The weather
was not propitious, one might say. Always plant your
corn the night after the full moon, and always wait until the time of ground frost is past. Otherwise the crop
will certainly prove to be stunted, at best.

Keeping to a steady pace, inasmuch as I anticipated
pursuit—though how determined it might be I didn't
know—I made my way to Bootjack and Mormon Bar.
I camped at the head of a narrow ravine, far up on a
ridge side, perhaps a mile or more away from the main
trail. It's best, after all, to err on the side of caution.
But as luck would have it, I was able to find a spring
that dribbled over a diorite face and pooled nicely at
the bottom. Until this point, Berutti had been somewhat cranky—but when I dismounted and unsaddled
him and led him to the catch basin, his spirits im-
proved considerably.

Well after nightfall I made a small fire to cook with,
extinguishing it when I was finished with my meal. In
the aftermath of all that had happened, I had genuine
difficulty in getting some sleep. My mind wouldn't turn
off, if you know what I mean. Then, when I finally
was able to drift into slumber, half a dozen coyotes on
the slopes below where I lay put up an ungodly yam-
mer. After that, a horned owl perched in a fir tree just
above me and began its distinctive hoo-hoo, hoo-hoo-
hoo. I tried to talk the bird into finding a different
flagpole, but he seemed determined to stick around.
For all I know there may have been a nest in the tree.

I awoke with dawn, forgot to check for the hooter's
nest, saddled Berutti and led him back downslope—
since I didn't want to take a chance, however slim, that
the big fellow might hurt a leg.

Before noon I was in Mariposa. Here I purchased such supplies as I might be able to carry in my saddle-bags, considered the purchase of a pack mule, decided against that plan, and continued northward to the Merced River crossing, at which point I turned up-stream, moving ahead slowly until I was beyond the farthest gravel deposits and hence beyond the final signs of mining operations. This portion of the water-shed was, according to received wisdom, barren—not so much as a color to a pan.

The canyon around me was extremely steep, rocky, and relatively free of vegetation—as though something in the formations discouraged plant growth. Indeed, one would almost suppose the canyon was about to play out against sheer cliff faces, but the flow of the river argued otherwise, for the current was considera-ble, the water a dark milky green shade, as though it fed from the high, snow-locked reaches of the great mountain range.

Only the faintest trail led along the river here, and intuition told me that the Indians were very careful in-deed not to reveal their comings and goings. The place was remote enough, God knew, but hardly sufficient to provide living space for a village such as Pohonichi was supposed to be. But for a very tired gambler, turned miner, turned (possibly) fugitive from justice, these few square rods of tufted grass and half a dozen riverside alders would provide an admirable camping site. Indeed, I found sign of a recent fire. Was this pos-sibly the very place where Ponwatchie and Manzanita had awaited Tenieya's scouts to come to them?

I would, I resolved, wait a day or two for Pon-watchie to show up. Even if Jamie chose not to give the man my message, he'd know where to find me. The danger lay in Mike Bonner and a couple of deputies tracking Ponwatchie. Bonner, it was said, could trail a jackrabbit across the lava beds around Mount Shasta. Well, the boys do love to exaggerate. If Ponwatchie exercised reasonable caution, nobody was going to tail him.

In any case, I guessed that Bonner wasn't likely to do any more than ride out a few miles, tell his deputies that I'd saved the town of Coarse Gold the cost of a trial and a hanging, and turn around. That was the likely scenario.

The greater danger, of course, would come from whatever of Piedra's men had been with him, no doubt camped not far from Coarse Gold itself, in anticipation of miners with full pouches, or better yet, a stage with a strongbox aboard. With their leader most definitely dead, what would his companyeros do? If they were practical-minded gents, they'd choose a new leader and be about their business. If they where loco with loyalty toward their fallen *patrón*, why, in that case I was subject to have some difficulty.

High above the grassy spit of land next to the surging Merced River, half a dozen vultures were circling, and with them a single condor, twice the size of the other big birds, at the very least.

Berutti waded out into the river, drank his fill, and then scrambled up the bank. He shook out his mane and tail, almost in the fashion of a huge, overgrown dog, and then bared his teeth at me.

"So what's with you, Mr. Horse?"

"Name's Berutti," he replied, "and don't you forget it. Boss, I don't suppose you'd be interested in taking a couple shots at those damned death chickens? Truth to say, they make me nervous."

"The big birds are no threat," I replied. "If I tried to drive them off, I might as well just inform the Indians that we're here—as well as anyone else who might be interested."

The stallion chewed at some grass for a moment and then looked up again.

"You're pretty sure the Little Apple still has Deuce with her, are you?"

I spread out my blankets, drank tepid water from

the canteen I'd been carrying, and lay down, put my hands behind my head.

"In this life, Berutti, a man can't really be certain of anything. You take whatever cards the Big Kay-hoona deals you, and you bluff a lot, and you play to win. And that, as they say, is the bottom line."

Possibly Berutti had nuzzled into an ant nest, I don't know. In any event, suddenly he was shaking his head back and forth and raising one foreleg so as to rub at his mouth with his hoof.

"You're a very strange horse, a very strange horse indeed," I told him.

"The pot," he replied, "calls the kettle black."

In truth, however, I'm not certain that's precisely what he did say. He was somewhat preoccupied with spitting out pismires, I guess.

Sixteen

VALLEY OF THE GRIZZLY BEAR

There was poor lame Claude, a hard old case,
Who never did repent;
Claude never missed a single meal,
Nor ever paid a cent.
But gambling Claude, like all the rest,
Did to Death at last resign,
For all in his bloom, at a hundred and ten,
In the days of 'Forty-nine.

But for Manzanita they had a bounty
And tried to track her down too,
They would have brought her in, that beauty,
And stretched her neck with hemp, so;
I took to the hills in hope I could find her,
And learned where Tenieya had his town,
Where streams leap down with a thunderous whine
In the days of 'Forty-nine.

And now my comrades all are gone,
Not one remains to toast;
They have left me here in my misery,
Like some poor wandering ghost.
And as I go from place to place,
Folks call me Ahaseurus:
And there goes Ace Tanner, a bummer sure,
From the days of 'Forty-nine.

Two days later Ponwatchie found his way to my campsite beside the swirling Merced River, and I must admit I was genuine glad to see the old cuss. But after he gave me the reconnaissance he had, I wasn't so certain.

All hell was about to break loose, or so my Indian friend seemed to believe.

"Don't know why they care about Jesus Piedra all of sudden, but after you left, some of his men come into Coarse Gold that night and demanded that Muddy Mike track you down, try you for murder. Said you killed Piedra an' three other guys too. Raised hell also. Bonner run 'em out of town, told 'em not to come back. Then, later, a fire got started, don't know how. But someone set fire to more buildings. Half damn town burn, everything on west side of Main Street. . . ."

I studied Ponwatchie's expression and thought about matters. The picture was beginning to fill in around the edges. I could envision Mike Bonner's nice tight little jail was gone, and I said a prayer to the effect that I trusted no one was locked in it at the time. The Savage Mercantile, fortunately, was on the east side of the street, so my cousin's investment at least had been saved, but Thompson's Watering Hole would be gone, as well as three or four other saloons and the Coarse Gold Bakery as well.

Ponwatchie continued: "Everyone thinks Tenieya's warriors done it, an' Joe at the livery says he saw what looked like some woman riding with a gang that might have been Yosemites. Bunch of fellows say she was wife to one of the Joaquins, while someone else says it was Joaquin Murieta. Me, I think One-eye Joe was drunk on ass. No Injuns for Christ sake. Next morning some of them bummers, the miners who never mine nothing, they crowded around outside where jail used to be. They want Cousin Jamie's militia to go find Tenieya, then hang the chief and Manzanita too. One guy, Charley Buckles, that mean one with the scar across face, he say you're involved, you an' Manzanita. Be good to hang both of you an' mebbe Tenieya too. Even Lafayette Bunnell, he wants to go after Tenieya. Mike Bonner, he tells 'em all to get on home, let him do his job. But they don' want to do that, and that's when Muddy Mike takes off his badge and tosses it into the street. Says he's going prospecting, hell with them all. That point I guess I should get out of Coarse Gold before the vigilante bunch decides to hang Ponwatchie since nobody else available. Real ugly, Ace. You ain't got no friends in that town, I tell you, not even your cousin now. Jamie, he's going to lead the militia. They already getting ready to ride when I left. Hundred of 'em, mebbe. But don't know where Tenieya's people are, not yet anyway."

I shook my head. "You sure," I asked, "the boys weren't just waiting for you to leave so they could follow? As for Jamie, that's his job, after all. It's bigger than he is, and he can't do a thing about it, not if he wants to be senator or governor someday."

Ponwatchie made half a dozen quick hand signs. A man didn't have to know the language to comprehend the meaning of those gestures.

The faithful Ponwatchie provided me with directions to Tenieya's secret valley back in the Sierra but at the same time informed me that he had no way of being certain the Yosemites were actually there—or, if they were, whether Manzanita was with them.

The secret valley, he explained, was the place out of which the Merced River flowed—the place where numerous streams come together. But the canyon below made passage extremely difficult—impossible for the white man's wagons, though not for men on horseback—men who were willing to dismount and lead their horses from time to time.

Ponwatchie was fairly certain he had not in fact been followed, but nonetheless we made a conspicuous departure from the campsite beside the Merced, choosing a tributary ravine that passed through occasional groves of huge trees, monstrous cedars I guessed them to be at that time, and immense, stately sugar pines that were, if less huge than the cedars, nonetheless a good bit taller, their tops flattened out, and from whose branches were suspended very large cones that looked from a distance to be some sort of fruit ready for harvest by none other than God Himself.

So, if you catch my drift, we followed this stream upward until we had reached an elevation of perhaps two thousand feet above the river, high into the dark forest of pine and fir that draped the entire upper slopes of the Sierra. Here at the very springs at the head of the drainage, there were mats of azalea bushes, still in full bloom, even though the season had by now passed from spring into summer. The blossoms filled the air with a delicate, sweet aroma, and the parklike openness of the forest made me suppose I was on the verge of entering into the Garden of Eden itself. From our vantage point we overlooked the long, winding canyon of the Merced and could see eastward as well to the ragged summits of the mountains, peak after peak still covered with snow from the previous winter, mountains moving off in single file, as it were, to the north and to the south. I'd always been puzzled as to why Jed Smith, years earlier, had described the entire formation as a single mountain, Mount Joseph, as he called it. Looking eastward from the rocky promontory where we now stood, I could almost imagine it that way—a single great wave in the earth's surface, the high eastward rim raggedly exposed and splashed with the snows of the years.

At this point we parted company, Ponwatchie to go his way, and I to go mine. The Yosemite would head back toward Coarse Gold, he said, and if he should indeed encounter my kinsman James Savage and his Mariposa Irregulars, he'd agree to act as their guide, but would mislead them to a hunting village site high on the San Joaquin River, an encampment that would show evidence of recent use, since Tenieya and his people had been there earlier that spring.

From the dust I was carrying, I paid Ponwatchie a generous salary, and the two of us shook hands. In truth, we had no way of knowing if we'd ever see each other again. There was nothing unusual about that situation, actually, not in California in those days. In point of fact, human life in general is that way—since the lightning strikes of its own volition and is indifferent to human designs or desires.

My own plans at this moment were, at best, indeterminate. If Manzanita were innocent of those things being charged against her, then I had the means to acquire a barrister of high reputation, and one way or another I'd see to it that any trial that might take place would do so in Sacramento or in San Francisco or Monterey, where justice tended to be a bit less capricious. Indeed, I could well imagine the miners of Coarse Gold finding it quite exciting and novel to hang a woman, without any real malice in the matter. And since Manzanita had made no secret of being Indian, what, after all, could the problem be? Wasn't the killing of predatory Indians well within the boundaries of the law?

But doubtless, in his own good time, one Claudius McCool would show up in Coarse Gold, possibly with Maybelle on his arm, and in that case he'd wish to know where his erstwhile partner and one-time apprentice in the card trade was hanging out. In the event that I had not returned to either Coarse Gold or to our claim on the Stanislaus, Ponwatchie agreed to undertake to guide Mr. McCool to Mr. Tanner.

After beating my way about the bushes for a couple of days, I descended from the forested ridges and made my way back to the Merced River, at a point perhaps fifteen miles upstream from where I'd earlier camped and where Ponwatchie had found me.

"About damned time we went downhill for a spell," Berutti complained. But I knew he was thinking about sweet grass and a long drink from the river.

"Peace, noble stallion," I replied. "Word has it we're about to find our way into paradise itself. Just a matter of letting the Uzmatis discover us."

Berutti whinnied and shook his head. "Is Deuce really going to be there, boss, or are you just pulling my leg?"

Once back to the river, I selected a likely spot and built a campfire somewhat larger than it needed to be—and somewhat earlier than I needed to cook dinner. I made a point of laying on a generous portion of big green fanworts that I had harvested in a shady creek bottom that led to the river. These sent aloft quite a satisfactory quantity of blue smoke—enough to catch the attention of any scouts who might be positioned along adjacent ridge spines.

We spent that night beside the stream, and I led Berutti out onto a gravel bar where the water was perhaps no more than six or eight inches deep, and I used a big rag to wash him down. Most horses aren't especially fond of water, you see, but Berutti had always been a horse of another color, a cat of a different stripe.

Less than twenty-four hours later I found myself surrounded by Indians. These were Yosemites, of this I was fairly certain, for I recognized two or three Miwok words, but my attempts to demonstrate friendliness went for naught. The warriors spoke hardly at all among themselves, and they spoke not at all to me—except, as I say, to let me know that I was their prisoner and that they would gladly do me in if I gave them the least excuse.

They relieved me of Johnny Mankiller, bound my hands, and led Berutti by means of a hackamore. We moved on foot, upstream, for perhaps eight or ten miles, gradually making our way to a point perhaps a thousand feet above the river. From there we began a descent and passed through several narrow aisles of standing granite into a spacious valley of stunning dimensions, its floor lush green and spotted here and there with pines and oaks, while the walls of the enclosed area were of sheer granite, formations of astonishing mass—bare, jagged stone, with occasional waterfalls leaping what I estimated to be as much as a thousand feet or even twice that in one instance. Never in my lifetime had I seen anything to match the utter spectacle of this place.

Thus was I ushered into the secret valley of the Yosemites, the Valley of the Grizzly Bear, as the name U-z-ma-ti itself indicated. If the high forests and immense trees I had seen a few days earlier suggested a nearness to the Garden of Eden, the primeval wilderness which lay at the very beginnings of human experience, this valley surrounded by immense cliffs was certainly that Eden itself, the fabled Garden of Creation—here inexplicably transposed into the mountains the Indians called Inyo.

Bound prisoner though I was, my breath was tight in my chest—because of the simple beauty, because of what seemed like the very presence of God Himself in this place. Perhaps I ought not to carry on this way, if you see what I mean, and yet it's true—as far as I know, it's true. This had to be the place Zenas Leonard described in his journal, a place found and then lost again for nearly twenty years, and I had become the first Boston, the first gringo, ever to stand on the floor of this most lovely and spectacular of all natural cathedrals on earth.

We approached an Indian village situated near the base of an astonishing waterfall, the wickiups formed of carefully cut branches interlocking above shallow pits in the ground and overlaced either with elkhide or with rabbit pelts sewn together and draped over willow boughs or the like.

Berutti was turned loose, and, faithless creature, he immediately set his nose in the direction of a grassy area where numerous other horses grazed. Or had he detected a familiar whinny?

In my mind's eye I could see the old thief prancing toward a particularly filly of his acquaintance, and after a huff and a whistle of recognition, rearing and oh so delicately mounting the lady in question.

But immediately I was taken to a lodge whose relative size denoted its importance and was roughly forced within. Here I was confronted by none other then Tenieya himself—the will o' the wisp leader of this band of Miwok Indians who were rumored to have the supernatural ability simply to disappear back into the mountains, to vanish, like so many sylphs from faery land. Having now entered into their secluded fortress, I understood precisely how such a rumor might find credence among the mining camps below.

In the lodge with us was a woman, the matriarch, as I supposed, and two girls who were still children. The three of them paid me no attention and went about the business of preparing food. These females, as I guessed, were Tenieya's family—though for all I knew, there may well have been several other children, adults perhaps.

The man himself, facing me here, was a muscular individual taller than most of the braves but an inch or so shorter than I. His face was strangely tattooed, as were his long, powerful arms, and around his neck was a string of what I took to be bear's teeth and the talons of eagles. His crownlike headdress appeared to be made of wildcat fur and was punctuated by several small tufts of red feathers, as from the shoulders of redwing blackbirds or the crests of woodpeckers.

I was surprised to note the man's eyes were gray, not brown. And his demeanor demanded attention. I met his gaze but, gambler though I was by trade, I had to force myself to do so.

"Who are you?" the head chief, the Toko Hayapo, demanded in clear English. "Tell my your name. Tell me why you were searching for our village. Tell me why you wished my men to find you. Only a fool builds a smoky fire in the late afternoon—or a man who wishes to be discovered."

I nodded, felt an unaccountable urge to clear my throat—almost as though I were back in Pennsylvania, in the seventh grade, let's say, and I had to give a book report, but without notes.

"My name's Jesse Tanner, though mostly folks call me Ace. And I've come here to find Manzanita Huerfano. My friend Ponwatchie told me how to reach you, Tenieya of the Yosemites, and I've got a message for you. Major James Savage and the other whites— the Mariposa Militia—are looking for this valley. Ponwatchie told me that he'd attempt to guide the militia in the wrong way, perhaps to a hunting village on the river my people call the San Joaquin. Some of the mining camps have been burned, and cattle have been stolen from the ranchos in the big valley. Perhaps the Chowchillas did these things, but the militia's looking for your people."

"That does not make sense," Tenieya replied. "Why is James Savage not searching for the Chowchillas? I could lead him to them if he asked me to do so. Why should my people have to be confined to a *ranchería* because of things the Chowchillas have done?"

"I can't answer your questions, Tenieya," I replied. "James Savage is my own cousin, and yet he's after me also. I killed a man named Jesus Piedra in a gunfight."

"And four other men as well," Tenieya said. "We keep ourselves posted if we can—what happens in the white villages ... Ponwatchie speaks with those who speak to me. If the militia searches for us, what will the militia do when it finds us? Do they wish us to make peace and then force us to live where they tell us to go?"

I nodded.

"You are Ace the gambler," Tenieya nodded. "The one you call Silver-leaf has spoken your name. She will be glad to see you."

"Manzanita?"

The chief gestured to one of his daughters, who quickly left the lodge—returning but a minute or so later with Manzanita herself.

I stared, as though dumbfounded, hardly recognizing this woman I loved, so complete had been the transformation. She was wearing a white deerskin skirt, but her breasts were bare—in the manner of the Yosemite people, and her long hair was unbraided and cascading over her shoulders. A thong of rawhide was about her neck, and that cord suspended the silver and turquoise coyote medallion that had become, in my mind, a symbol of her very being.

"I . . . I came to ask you to marry me," I managed. "Jesus Piedra is dead. He attacked me . . . I had no choice, Manzanita. I killed him."

"Don't apologize to me, Gringo Tanner. It has been a long time since I could bear to be around that man—no, that swine, that *porco*. I would have killed him myself if I'd had a weapon—when he tried to. . . ."

I stood there, stupidly looking at her, attempting to take in the degree of transformation. This woman who stood before me—she appeared utterly at ease with herself, someone who belonged to another world than the one I lived in. Perhaps I'd never before truly thought of her as Indio.

Hands on hips, Manzanita was scowling at me.

"Why are you staring at my breasts?" she demanded. "When a woman looks at a man, she searches his eyes. The same should be true of a man who has just asked a woman to marry him."

God help me, I felt myself blushing. I grinned.

"You're beautiful," I said. "Forgive me. I couldn't

help myself. We males of the species are incorrigible, but if God didn't want us to admire 'em, then why'd He give 'em to you?"

"How do you answer this man, Silver-leaf?" Tenieya demanded. "You have hardly stopped speaking of him since you came here to live among us, and now you wish to have word battle with him? If you desire this man, you may have him. Otherwise I will call to the young warriors, and they will take him outside my lodge and kill him."

Manzanita grinned, her eyes full of mischief.

"Let me think about it," she replied. "Has this man brought a bride price, Tenieya?"

It had crossed my mind, actually, that the Yosemite chief might possibly just be toying with me. Perhaps he had in mind to use me as a hostage—it would give him something to bargain with, if and when the Mariposa Militia made contact. I thought about the derringer pea-shooter tucked into my boot, but that weapon, I realized, wasn't going to do my a hell of a lot of good.

"How can I marry this man, Tenieya?" Manzanita continued. "To whom would he pay the bride price, even if he had one?"

"Manzanita, Claude and I, we struck it rich on the Stanislaus," I blurted. "I'm a rich man, so to speak, and the claim's a long way from being worked out. What do you need, Tenieya? I can obtain things for you, things that your people will be able to use. . . ."

"Will you buy us guns, Ace Tanner?" Tenieya asked. "Then we would be able to defend ourselves against this Mariposa Militia."

"No one," Manzanita burst in, "will be able to take a bride price from this man. He's the one who owns me. Twice he has gambled and won, and several times he's protected me and saved my life that way. This man already owns me, and I do not choose to dispute his claim."

There might have been a shred of a trace of a smile on Tenieya's face, but then the chief controlled himself.

"In that case, you are already married. Take your husband and go, Silver-leaf. I have different business to attend to now. I must go down to the whites, to the Saldu, because there is no other choice. The young men may wish to fight, but I think we must do what the white man says. I have already spoken with the commissioners, and they say the war between us can only be over when we will consent to live on a *ranchería*."

With these words Tenieya turned and exited from the lodge, leaving me alone with Manzanita—and of course Mrs. Tenieya and her two daughters. I realized they had hesitated in their work and that their eyes were now upon Manzanita and me.

We embraced, kissed. Then I held her momentarily at arm's length, glanced at the chief's wife and her daughters, and then impulsively bent forward and touched my lips to the nipple of each of Manzanita's breasts.

Manzanita laughed. "The man always wants to nurse as his child might nurse," she said. "Male children never wish to give up nursing. Females have much more sense in this matter."

"How did you get so damned smart?" I demanded, folding her into my arms.

"At the mission," she said, "*voy a estudiar latín en la clase*. That is how. And I do not use double negatives in *inglés* either, no matter what you say, Gringo Tanner, not unless I want to."

We were still laughing when Tenieya reentered the lodge. There was a look of concern on his face, and of inevitable acceptance.

"My scout," he said, "tells me your friend James Savage and his men have already reached the lower canyon of the Merced. Perhaps it is true that he thinks my people are the ones who burned and murdered, rather than our friends the Chowchillas. I will try to talk with your cousin, Ace Tanner, for I've heard that he's a reasonable man. What shall I tell him when he asks me where you are, for he is bound to inquire? Perhaps the white man's law will protect you, but will it protect Mayenu-osa-be also? I do not think the white law will protect a woman who is Miwok. I think you two must go the other way. You must cross over the Inyo, beyond where the streams begin, and go on to the bad-water lake on the east side, for I do not think your own cousin will follow you to that land. Tenieya has friends among the Mono, a man who is Echuto Hayapo among his own people. Once, years ago, we met near the top of the mountains when we were both hunting. At first we thought we would have to fight, but instead we became friends and hunted together. I will give you my token, and you must give it to the one called Wolverine with Bad Feet."

"You do not intend to fight the white men, Tenieya?" Manzanita asked.

Tenieya gestured with both hands—indicating his family, his home, all the others who lived in the village of Pohonichi.

"Would it do us any good? Eventually the Saldu would find us, even here, and then they would kill all of us, and our people would go into darkness. Perhaps one day the whites will leave our land, and then we will be able to return, I don't know. I am old—I feel very old today, even though I am only a little bit older than this Yankee gambling man you have married, Silver-leaf. But soon there must be someone else to lead the people. We must trust in the future, for there is nothing else that we can trust. Yet now we will have to leave our beautiful valley, this place the Great Dreamer prepared for us at the very beginning of time, this place which Coyote howled into existence because the Dreamer had told him to do so. The white man cannot harm our special place, so it will be here when in some future time the Uzmati Miwoks are allowed to return. We will not know that time, but perhaps our great-

great-grandchildren or their great-great-grandchildren will know it."

With Manzanita Huerfano giving directions, a dozen or more of the Yosemites made preparations for a journey across the high granite mountains to the east, to a hoped-for refuge with the Monos in the high desert lands beyond the Inyo.

Tenieya went with his scout to talk to the whites, and when he returned the following day, his eyes were dull and lifeless.

"We must go to a *ranchería* near the San Joaquin River," he said. "We must leave this valley of the grizzly bear."

Manzanita and I and the dozen or so Yosemites who had elected to accompany us bid goodbye to friends and relatives, and we all began a trek into a different world, one in which, we hoped, the white men would never wish to dig for gold—or anything else. I knew better, of course, but this was not the time to say so.

When the sun rose above the Inyo, a thin silver disk that burned white fire, we were already out of the valley itself. We stood atop high cliffs overlooking the floor of the relatively small but magnificent valley. We gazed down, and once again I was awestruck by the amazing beauty of this place that Coyote had "howled into existence."

A column of whites had already entered Yosemite Valley from the canyon below. The group had come to a halt, and I knew why. Jamie and the others were stunned by these amazing vistas, just as I had been—and just as Zena Leonard had been years earlier, staring from the snow-locked heights into that placid green oasis where springtime was in full blast, even though the mountains were yet locked in their Siberian winter.

Manzanita dismounted from Deuce and walked over to stand beside me, there on the edge of the precipice.

"What kind of life lies ahead for us, Ace Tanner?" she asked.

"With luck," I replied, "perhaps a pretty good one."

She nodded. "The magic of my coyote medallion will protect us," she said.

Then we two, our lives all before us, whatever those lives might entail, mounted Berutti and Deuce, respectively, and hurried to catch the small band of Yosemites who had chosen to strike out for a desperate freedom rather than to accept the relative security and truncation of freedom that life on a *ranchería* would entail.

For ourselves, we were passing, not down out of Eden, but up and away from the Garden, and the sky overhead on this day of our emancipation was immense and blue. Only above the crests of the Sierra were a few ragged cumulus towers beginning to form.

The Indians, as I made note, had chosen not to look back.

EPILOGUE:
WHAT MAY
HAVE
HAPPENED TO
JESSE

Right after I finished this present reworking of Jesse
Tanner's journal, I took a little expedition south to
Silver Mountain. Most of the snow was gone by
late June, and after a couple days of traversing the
mountain, I stumbled onto what had to be the cabin—
the very place where my own grandpa met Ace hisself
and was subsequently given the journal. Perhaps I
hoped to find Manzanita's coyote medallion hanging
from a nail inside the cabin, or something of the sort,

but that didn't happen. The greater mystery, however, had to do with Jesse's fate. He surely hadn't set up a death lodge, in the manner of the Indians, but what had come to pass?

What was necessary, or so I told myself, was just a matter of using my noodle so as to think like a hundred-year-old man who's riding a mule. Come to find out, it wasn't all that hard.

But before I get to the issue, which is the main point of this here scholarly epilogue, there are a couple of details that Jesse left out—or at least didn't put in as distinctly as he might have.

First off, Chief Tenieya did indeed make contact with James Savage and his Mariposa Militia, pleading that the Uzmatis should be allowed to live at peace in their mountain valley, but the appeal was to no avail. As an officer of the state, volunteer or otherwise, James Savage saw it as his beholden duty to make the mountains safe for gold miners, and that meant of course just one thing for the Indians: life on a *rancheria*, a supervised area too small to be called a reservation. In California in those days, land granted to Indians was kept to a minimum, naturally, because one never knew where gold was likely to be discovered next. Anyway, Tenieya was allowed to return to his people for the purpose of escorting them in, which he agreed to do.

When James Savage, Lafayette Bunnell, and the rest of the Mariposa Battalion finally made their way into Yosemite Valley, guided by Tenieya himself, white men looked for the first time upon that magic cathedral of the Sierra—though, as Tanner notes several times, Joe Walker, Zenas Leonard, and the others almost certainly peered from the cliffs above as they made their way across the snow-choked mountains some eighteen years earlier.

James Savage never got to be governor, or senator either, but Jesse and Manzanita had a long life together in ways that might surprise you, traveling a considerable portion of the Old West and having quite a few hair-raising adventures. A lot of what they did is recorded in Tanner's journal, complete with details of the further exploits of Johnny Mankiller and the noble Berutti, and it could be I'll get around to working another novel or two after a time.

But back to the subject at hand.

Accounts of the magic place we now call Yosemite spread rapidly after Savage and his men made their report, and so it was merely a matter of time until the coyote who howled the valley and the waterfalls and all the rest into existence had managed to find among the Saldu that one individual whose vision and whose voice would advertise Yosemite to the world and ultimately pressure the government into including the place within a great national park. That man, of course, was John Muir, *John O' Mountains*.

Hetch-Hetchy, the little Yosemite, got its bottom filled with swamp water backed behind concrete, for the benefit of San Francisco. Perhaps eventually we'll come around to undoing that particular crime against nature, and Muir will be able to rest comfortably in his grave.

It's a puzzle why we have to build dams, allow cows to graze, permit mining activities and the like, even inside our national parks. Doesn't make sense.

But about the other issue:

Grandpa Ward never followed Jesse Tanner when Ace rode off on his mule, or at least that's what was claimed. Me, I wasn't so certain about that. Grandpa Ward was fascinated by puzzles, as I recall. In any case, I'd already spent several days wandering the slopes of Silver Mountain, and a few more weren't going to hurt. So, as I say, I thought like a hundred-year-old man on a mule, and eventually I found myself at a small, grassy bench at the foot of three considerable rocky towers. An adit ran back into the mountain at that point, and anyone could see a good deal of mining activity had taken place over the years. Tanner had caught a good case of gold fever when he was working that claim on the Stanislaus, and so it was inevitable he'd start digging even after he retired, so to speak, to Silver Mountain. According to the journal, that's where he took Manzanita when she died.

In truth, I nearly missed what I came to find—and the clue to that was what remained of a piece of sap-laden white pine such as might have been used for a nameplate on a home-dug grave. What was still faintly visible: Mayenu-osa-be, Manzanita Huerfano's Yosemite name, which probably meant something like "woman chief" or "wife of the chief," even though neither thing had been true. The Yosemite people, like quite a few other groups, gave their young ones names that had power. If her parents hadn't been killed, of course, and if the girl hadn't ended up at the mission, things likely would have been a good deal different all the way around.

Manzanita's grave, I suspected, was close by the opening to the mine shaft, beneath a grove of quaking aspens—because I found a leaf-covered mound that proved to be composed of fist-sized rocks, possibly put in place to keep away vultures, bears, coyotes, badgers, and whatnot.

Below the spring and the aspen grove is a slope composed of loose stone, talus—part of it mining debris, part natural. Something caught my eye, and so I climbed down to the foot of the scree. There, scattered among the rocks, were a number of bone fragments and a badly rusted pistol, the metal completely corroded, handle missing, and so forth. In fact, I couldn't tell what kind of six-shooter it had been. In a moment of blinding surmise, however, I could see Ace Tanner taking his own life—because, after all, it was clearly time to go. I picked up the now useless old weapon, held it in my hand, and could almost hear the thing chuckling to itself, just as Jesse said it did. The ghost of Johnny Mankiller.

I took the gun with me, but otherwise touched nothing there at the supposed resting place, and headed back to the sagged-in remains of the cabin. The hour was close to sundown when I got there, intending to spend the night before returning to civilization—and to the writing of this epilogue.

But in the alpenglow, sitting side by side on what remained of the cabin's front stoop and looking for all the world as though they had good sense, were two coyotes, male and female by the size of them—what we call High Sierra coyotes, twice the normal weight and longer in the legs, creatures I suspect that are actually coy-wolves. Anyhow, they're good-looking animals, long-limbed and as large as big dogs. The two of them sensed my presence immediately, and they watched me intently as I trudged the slope toward the ramshackle cabin. I had a distinct feeling the coyotes had no intention of deferring to any mere human, though it's possible, I suppose, that they actually knew who I was.

Jesse and Manzanita?

Then, when I was no more than fifty or sixty feet from the canines, they lazily stood up, wagged their tails, touched noses, and glided off into the dark forest of red firs and piñons surrounding the little meadow where a cabin continues to stand, despite the heavy snows of a century or so.

Anyhow, I decided not to stay the night. I gathered the few things I'd packed in with me, and with the aid of a battered, U.S. Forest Service–issue flashlight (itself now nearly forty years old), I made my way from the mountain to the trailhead, where I'd parked my gray 'eighty-three Thunderchicken a few days earlier.

Eventually I took the rusted-up pistol to a gunsmith friend of mine, a fellow who's a genuine expert with regard to identifications of this sort, and he concluded the weapon was indeed a Colt-Patterson revolver, just as I guessed it was when I found it.

Anyhow, I've got Jesse's pistol sitting right here on my desk, where I use the thing as a paperweight. As to Grandpa Ward's four-ten, why that's standing in the corner behind me. Every once in a while I use it to celebrate the New Year or to shoot at my neighbors, if they happen to rile me.

    So long for now & stay on the good side of the Big Coyote,

Bice Hotchkiss

June 24, 1994